Private Martial Artists

Private Martial Artists

Mixed Up in It

Mattee Kraus

To order additional copies of this book, contact:
Xlibris
1-888-795-4274
www.Xlibris.com
Orders@Xlibris.com
792171

One

Hail Bums (adventurous martial arts)

The party had been rolling and the group were there.

Mimi and Minnie, often party hosts at their houses, included concerns in their talk.

Mimi said, "He had given it to me as a payment with uh storage the running ruining the stove that was in the house so it was not completely ruined. I was never to use a stove again for years. The only such appliance I would have available would be the hot plate."

Minnie, who was listening commented, "I was rather feeling it's at that next to a nest of a room, not to mention that the previous tenant was a policeman. I had assumed or the landlord had, many years, he may have felt I have recently or end at this other friend. had. he left an average roadmap I will take him a roadmap and drink it with a paper rash more last for ich ard beautiful change for of possibly another nature and possibly it was just sort of thing that allowed me to write another story or two reason the truth is it's rationality."

"I was writing to apply to some of my favorite short stories all my true friends were all mixed up and I shouldn't have been so mad at my gift-giving friend a television set was real nice and he hadn't destroyed the relationship. But at the time I was perhaps working on a slightly different psychotic, subconscious level."

"I had time." said Dr. Portini. "I told my friend to come back who has seemed to be here or not destructive disturbing our incessant ap od line at times and bordered on until four in the morning. It was much too much! I was to consider my actions and in the meantime it's been for small change, too small an amount."

Buzzy, who hadn't been there in a while, appeared and sat near Boozy.

Buzzy said, "The television set had once been hooked up, only temporarily, it wasn't right. It was fixed by a neighbor friend, but you know I'm not paying for that. If it's your system, it's your fault. Even it if was new, even though new, it was through telling me and you things."

Mimi said, "I wasn't paying for it, but I could get the stations even without the hook up. Sometimes I couldn't and after a little bit I'd watch the snow like fuzz lines on the screen. That's electricity through the eyes of a picture tube."

Boozy said, "But as it was other end again I meant my friend it I told not to come back and everything seemed to be okay and yet he would be back a few more times which I really really hardly only welcomed I was hoping that he liked it."

Buzzy said, "I had probably forgotten to ask for non-appearance there, but they had it, I had made the request a few times too many. So when he returned we were spreading nuts and washers out over quite a wide piece of paper. Then, while they sat there and he wasn't bringing his friend with him, this turned on time stretched out to a few years. If it hadn't been for any of his friends, who would have paid a ship's ransom to be there, you would be the only person sitting here right now."

Dr. Portini came to the party.

Dr. Portini commented, "I would have told my worker that and I'd be somewhere else."

Buzzy went on, "Me and that friend of yours were right about, it wasn't your day. He was there and we had it with him."

"I suspected that he was a scientist too." Mimi said.

Dr. Portini supposed, "He was like he was, after this one time when I was ill, it lasted too long, he was like perhaps someone. He was with the movies that were so on my mind."

Buzzy said, "She's even in college."

It was like the next day continuing, which continued with people coming in.

Boozy came to the cottage and knocked. Mimi let him in and he got comfortable on the sofa. Buzzy looked at him.

"What brings you to here?" asked Mimi.

Boozy replied, "I went on. Then three days at a time passed. My television, which helped keep me company eventually malfunctioned, so I moved on. I said, to Mimi, you have to give in to the all and I'll get back to you."

"Me," Zoong replied. "I am out of here. Too bad you missed Mimi."

"He was off the phone, off the cable, and it was all off my mind." replied Boozy "The service to be it seemed that family."

"Finally was what I was, still in touch with that don't come back frame of reference." Boozy said. "And Buzzy had had it. It being early morning, he was one time that was the right time that was right on. And we was right on."

Dr. Portini, included empathy and commented, "And once about the last time you saw him, when you had had a rough day at the job."

Boozy said, "I was working at a farm and he was coming home. It was good to see your friend's face."

The mind wars were what they had once been. They seemed to be okay with that.

"And when I was still in a hectic confusion for some reason or another," said Boozy, "it had got to me."

Dr. Portini helped out, "The drift of that is this. We had gone to a good time and we were spending so much time there at the party, and this didn't fit into my sort of thinking, one day went to the next week."

Boozy, as usual, replied, "Because he was into this sort of thing, he didn't have any definite evidence, conclusive or otherwise, about anything."

"We'll tell it was them or not, it wasn't wrong about that time after I said goodbye to my friends. That's to be."

"Everything worked so good, fortunately. It seemed fortunate. it still seemed good that we left early, though. Was good to go through time before, and I was all and all and ready, so it didn't much matter. Working, and it's so warm multiplying the rays, it's because that's where was friendship again."

"So It might be copulating for all I know?" said Bonozy Neo.

Booxy, relaxed, started talking, "From alls I know, perhaps it had something to do with my psychotic tears for you. As the day, I might have been reminded of the years and I knew when not to, so that they were probably more expensive past perhaps and camping days for me were there. And less after when I slept there would up swans of the ice chests. would like when the fish would run up the steam for days."

"But other times when I lived there, later tonight, one could and would do him tricks. Far from my house for my bedroom I would here than there were a couple of very all of it working one of the private rooms was in an easterly direction. So it was that at times, origination had or so had there was two story."

"To put lights on around midnight to breakfast. And begin again. I may have considered it possible that I was doing the waiting or perhaps, in this, account retrieving.

Old, most of the similar dates in nature are to those I will reserve, as one. And appreciating them being convinced of their value, I was at home with randoms, so for about two years or so, I mean, I didn't have a lady. I know from the account of two and a half years ago."

"A nearness of strangers, I guess."

"Reminds me of a nearby thoroughfare. It will be a good two years before I'm over."

"Above ground, that time I had another as you unfortunately in rain, who is too; and seizure. I was into her later when being sober was in personal contact. I was impressed with her and suddenly shocked at the report of his death."

The man who had been working and working had left over to some other place. He'd come there up to four times.

Boozy said, "He shared his own up with me older of line of days what you heard down by your older talented old older align have been already now my friend or friends I should say I had left it was a friend and his wife so he was overbearing. But I'd hardly be helpful if responsible people I had noticed were it. As I was separate from the gang, all poor household as it was and due to several reasons being the most prominent though mine."

"Did Boozy come to be a part of the event?" Asked Mimi.

Buzzy replied, "Yes, but in terms of the pass to complex."

A party! The party that the psychotic was into did happen. It was a gender disorientation foundation. It went from a friend mate, as male-female- as black-white, declaring to another friend, doing a dance, that going to another place, another party, another time or even to the original place, where the personal gender disorientation psychosis of id person, the male psychotic being part of their mind as the female part of their mind dreamt, which wound up having a pretty good time.

Yet they went to a party. And so on top of that, the party that they were at was where the group mentality went single. It was the same gender schizoid psychosis moment that the party about the horizon ascribed to.

"You have to pay a sum." said Minnie Mu, the party's apparent receptionist.

Death walked, waited and wandered it seemed. The hailer person was a surprise but different.

"Boozy wanders." said Minnie to Dr. Portin in private after witnessing it.

Dr. Portini pried, "Boozy was a case. So was it Boozy?"

"It was a good at a party thing."

The party went on."

"The party walked and talked to me." explained Minnie.

And as he had accepted the experience as of a moderate cocktail party falling-out once, as it was with Boozy, who liked the experience, it was with everyone. It was a bit off as it was so dramatic. It was but a test trance for living. Dr. Portini waited before asking the next question.

He said, "Boozy! Was it a temporary experience for both of you? Yes, sure it was!"

And when they had all left and gone to their homes, cabin assignments, stopping for shopping for nic-naks at some makeshift coffee houses transpired and they went to where they had been before.

Boozy had come from across town. Boozy stopped before getting home across the park. He pulled over his vehicle, which was borrowed from Minnie's friend, into his parking lot and paused.

For a moment he looked out the window as a way to reflect on being transient, then got a feeling given to him from being at the group therapy party. He was elated. Call out to that guy across the street, who looked familiar, who looked like one of the people he worked with, maybe it was from on the job the other job the year before.

"This was being at the party," he said, ruminating out loud to no one. "It was because the party was a place to relax the mind. As I was at the party.

"The party hailer nerved me." said Mimi.

This was losing it for Mimi. She had never said such a thing before and yet here it was, complaining. The party never was someone unusual, a person yet was nerving Mimi. Hail Mimi.

"Hello, Mimi." the party nerve hailer said.

"I'm nerved." Mimi said to her friend.

Being nerved at a party when relaxing and enjoying friendship company was not wanted by Mimi, nor would most any one want to be so nerved.

One check out of the party, whether group therapy or it goes on to another on going party, and I'm at the party again. It was just a group therapy!"

So the party flashback came up to his mind.

"And other friends were okay with it, sympathizing with it a little, which did nothing to help. Parties are okay with all the friends I have there." continued Boozy.

They would all go home. He had thought, someone would take some of them home.

He continued, "And their if their id, pseudo psycho, family was of mind there, the party was over."

Back at the party, Buzzy's friend continued the group therapy with an open question.

He said, "He was the psychotic person, who was with the id of inclusion of time being there. Did it bother you?"

Bonozy's friend was a virtual master at dream group therapy psychoanalysis, manipulating minds to enjoy their gender disorientation. They enjoyed their place of mind no matter, the town not of concern, not a city or love affecting, but close to leaving. And with their bags, before their enjoyable schizophrenic mind left them, while they had left their schizoid mentality in a town, which was a memorable way and left them starting to play games, it was okay they left. And they left. And so someone would be going there. And someone was there to be with. The best wishes of the schizophrenic person accompanied the relationship, which was a good time, and it was creative with relative time as it's possibly part pre craziness.

"I didn't realize it," said Minnie, "Until about these times, having a habitual partying experience was a problem with me. And that sort of took me into a job here of helping with rehabilitation of it. That wasn't into a so easy way. And great changes were along the way for me too."

Boozy spoke, "Yes, there might have been that thought, it was a party to haunt me, but grace is always being kind. And though it's demanding nothing, it's so fatalistic for a while being at a group therapy, group therapy, which had its rewards. It's rewarding for a while is rewarding."

The next day party did come down. It was a party of many of those who had been at it for over a year and a half and was sort of a celebration.

Then, Bonozy, who had left and returned to his room, came, much enthused, with Mimi, whose learned assist attitude was of friendliness. From there he would, so Mimi had set up for him, sooner than he thought, go to live for a while in a commune. It would be sort of like home. At their home as it had been, Mimi had got his paperwork started.

Then, Mimi would come and stay with him after a while.

For a while, they was getting along, and Buzzy's friend, from the new home, who had next to nothing and four friends, called to no one in particular.

Bo Nozy said, "Hey!" And he swung his knife upwards right in front of Mimi, who quickly jumped back.

Bo Nozy was a practicing theoretical physicist who had two papers published.

Bo Nozy, the person newly there said, "O.K. Which of you friends were being used?"

Boozy said, "Not me."

Bo Nozy replied, "Some of us, me included." As it was, those had something to say, who had wanted to say it were at the very least there, and they were feeling much feelings as of the friendship high psychosis." Boozy replied, "It nearly pulled me into gauging apprehensions of it. Us, we all got to be going and it pulled away after a little while."

Bo Nozy spoke up, "We were all all getting like my buddies; and my buddies' buddies were for a couple weeks just us. And man, in the next few years, it would go on like that. This one time, and I would quit my job after a few days, we were at another wonderful job. l and Minnie, we still worked another time. And quit after a few weeks. It was a good system for several summers."

Boozy commented, "Though not particularly good for us."

Bo Nozy added, "I was about on the job where I had smoked and I quit that good. It ended my job for me. And two of my friends also had lost their jobs when they had up and quit.

Boozy said, "Party on to after love room house."

"Somehow I just feel how much you love those are the type of people who might be reaching my thoughts at the most appropriate level for alignment of thinking experiences." Bo Nozy commented.

"On my party." said Mimi.

"The radio usually turns on by itself. It acts as if it is used to being turned on by such things as movements" complained Minnie.

"That's through a coincidence, they say." replied Mimi.

"There are pieces of the next to none of which bothering me." said Minnie.

Boozy wandered over to where the two girls were talking and said something off the wall. Bo Nozy was nearby and listening.

"I wonder who the real people are." said Bo Nozy.

Boozy replied, "And I remember, that they are probably there."

She probably had all their stuff under control without forgetting whose table she was at. Well of someone's got to have, just how much it is used really is, it's to make it, as it is, successful. That is out. But it is what it is. Probably just an overnight caller.

"There, that seems about the same as I remember, when you said, I am talking when I am not talking." Boozy said.

"I'm all over the place." answered Boozy. "But?"

"Or is someone giving me what seems like a lot of double talk about what he is doing. And when I finally become hungry for that real stuff in life, which is driving me nuts, I listen."

Boozy added on, "And so, when you had rule books to wear out, and if that is not enough, seats. Can't psychology and you go so there might have been something to see. My doctor says, 'she must have been okay'. And that will bring an old girlfriend to call. That would eventually have it's good side. Got little to say to the dog catcher, who had that uniform."

Music at college have been too cold, on the one hand, so folk music orientation and two. All classes and jobs worked. And then a first book was read.

Boozy said, "My enjoying the company of a, go get very special, teacher, was at least she and l see eye to eye."

Mimi commented, "She was okay to me. I apply until I graduate, and more than just when. She and sensuous friend Minnie are here. With all that a little lined up, we appreciated art, though a little more of it was a lot of there where there was effort."

"I hadn't realized." started Boozy.

There was silence.

A house party was basic. An info party, which was a not too recent memory of Minnie's, had been a way she could add less to the confusion of a house party. To one attending an average psychotic like party, one who was speculating in vain, the party was a gift from God. Either at a house party or an info party, of which many were on a baseball game, a sub party at the house party, which was in this case so it was into baseball trivia, where one who was spectating in vain, since there was no actual ongoing baseball game, it was comfortable to let things pass. So the house party was open to all.

Minnie, yet exclaimed, despite it being a nice house, "This is it. We're in a nice, clean, chaperoned party house. It's a way to sanity."

The freshly showered, well-dressed Doctor Portini, who was also a professional chaperone, considered his role at the party. Considering all the doctors that could have come there, Dr. Portini was rated as one of the highest. He said many things to Minnie.

He said, "Let's stay into yesterday at the house party? Can we talk about that? Is it too much?"

"Guess it's entirely a dormant evening come to early repose." replied Mimi.

Dr. Portini was somewhat disappointed that she had little to say. Boozy had heard and commented.

"Grass is what you want." Boozy said.

As the psychotic person told one 'Leo' of their elder-gender people, who were going through with their gender reassignments, which was where it was very clearly in attendance to the true place of what that was, Bo Nonzy called out, as the gender psychotic of the place.

Leo said, "Hey, Mimi, Bo Nozy, Boozy."

Bo Nozy, absent minded, echoed, "Hey, you guys."

Mimi said, "I am considering it, but it might be better something else."

Dr. Portini said, "The rehab, which had an alertness about it, is somewhere where the gender psychotic person can remain in their seat and experience moments of rotation, on that type of chair. This had little effect on gender orientation."

Like an owl sitting on a branch, little did the psychotic person realize it was but they were in psychosis. People, who formed the least of the few were in all. Before then and again many years later, realizing it was all in all they, who had taken those first steps, the people took it the few places where those whom they had been before were the same gender.

The psychotics, who were good people, and Doctor Portini who had the experience of being late so they would not have to go nuts enough, were well taken in by the invited doctors, some who were with their own gender disorientation professed Hippocrates and kept their heads up. And those psychotics, who had gone on their way after being interviewed, were stunned mentally by having returned to find the bulk of their orientation to gender consciousness was an experience in which the doctor could be in control. Guests mostly went camp to escape the whole lot of doctor control.

In camping, which required stopping a lot of normal, healthy living habits, they could go to a well for water. A group at a well-side taking drinks of their water had used the cups they brought with them. Others were provided there. They left them there.

They became more oriented on gender identification, became the people gender oriented people related to, and identified with the norm for long after the time they had gone to get a cup of water, where they were for a time.

At a group therapy the next day, this was a help, the doctor started by describing a situation.

Dr. Portini asked, "Do you see that these psychotics were bumming a classification from the doctor as to their specific psychosis, which was usually gender oriented?"

Boozy replied, "Yes, I see that. But it also seems possible this is normal."

By the time they identified a place to go in the session, the feelings they had, which usually took them to the back of their minds, had taken them back to the self conscious thought of gender. There, their subconscious was saying this to them, 'it is not a collective unconscious of gender based psychotic people, it's a self assessed collective subconscious of that, which does fit them since that is good to that psycho positives that crowd the subconscious'.

"As most of you know, the id of a psychotic person, who doesn't feel anything like a normal person who is the bumming norm, is a framework in which you all exist." said Dr. Portini.

"Do you fit in?" asked Mimi.

There was a long wait.

"Experience tells us a lot, friends. Experience takes us away from this sort of definition. But experience relies on it. I am one who is able to come back to terms in my id, with life. Life experiences are just a side time off. And I'm sure you can have that time off too." said Dr. Portini.

Then came the reply.

"What?"

There was a small education note for family gender orientation through subconscious collectives, family and gender could be especially related, on a poster on the wall there.

And since someone of the gender would go into it for the money, they risked short thoughts. It was, it used to be a buying point for the length of being unhurt.

There were others, but someone decided to call the bluff. The bum hailer was outside and to him fun was hailing blind. He didn't know who he was hailing, but he was hailing.

The hail came to Buzzy as he was walking up the walkway to the front door.

The bum hailer stood in the near shadow, not to be recognized unless the person he was hailing stopped and took a moment.

Two

In Martial Arts, Some Misadventure Anxiety Goes To Therapy

For Buzz (Boozy), hailing someone who had a safe compassion was in.

Someone who was an ex stoner like Chum Dring, who was asking for a joint party experience and finding peace In it, it was there no matter if it was difficult. But for Buzz, who was with the dream of a companion who could be with him in an inclusion of going to a group therapy with persons of a similar interest, the work of martial arts were mixed up. He was Kut Tuf if all he did was swing, but he also boxed, which was not even allowed by the Kut Tuf folks.

There was an exhibition and Buzzy watched. Chum was there too. He like this, Chum had people he saw and he took his acquaintances with him to exhibitions.

It was not so okay for Boozy, occasioned as Buzzy. So why hail someone when they are not so in a way, quite chummy? This was asked by many of the ex stoners at a party he went to.

Hailing a dream companion was so ex stoner that it was likely unreal. A party helped someone find peace of mind. So In group therapy- if one is hailing the person, it matters in a way if they are responsive.

Chum is the one with an answer. Chum says, say a hail and all will be well.

As those who hail are bums, and for those who are bums and are often hailed, being hailed is such a drag. That those who hailed such bums were a wonder since they are hailing bums was mixed up.

Chum was struggling with his own hesitation to work and earn bread when he hailed someone for some spare change. The man he hailed was normal looking, probably a working man on his day off.

Chum said, "Can you spare a dime?"

"Hey, you." the man commented as he stopped and reached in his pocket for some spare change.

Fighting in fame and well-knowingness was unlike other type of endeavors. The bums, they are not pure bums but professional fight hangers on declaring their affiliation to fight in court for side referentials that are usually given only to the licensed fighter, were recommended. Chum had his day.

Fight for self defense bummed the boxer! He was mixed up with martial arts characters and this got him into seeing a professional mental health practitioner.

Chum was bumming martial arts tips like nobody's business for a few years. Some tips came inside the space of five minutes by some acquaintance. Five minutes that could also be used to bum a dime were spent listening to the tip on how to self defend one's self.

A tip can and probably will be forgotten. But forgotten to the collective unconscious or the person's subconscious to reappear at will was it. If it's will, it was, while being highly unlikely a concern for the counselor Chum went to see for his problems, it mattered. Some of being over tipped with regard to crazy mixed up martial art self defense methods meant he was handicapped in his ways and practices.

Some are a little different since prestige is easy to get. Just need a board, maybe some breaks, and a trunk to put some clothes in.

"Hailing is," Zong once said, "a person on a bum. I'm in the 'my' position of one going to catch the bum who is as preparing to get in my private room. And they may declare to the other(s) who threaten to disregard their 'my' position of being bum catcher, perhaps disregarding safety and being in the way, that 'I go on and try to catch such a bum'."

He went on and described it further, "Take the bum, who had waited, hailed someone, and not gone somewhere. He had been where a considerable amount of sporty hailing had been going on. He was the athlete, semi-pro. He leaned into the support of peers for support, especially with regard to his status as a fine bum in crazy mixed up martial arts and was a self defense practitioner. They are the critic. There's one criteria that would surpass need for hailing, and that is silence."

But it required being in the know of how to practition across the gulf between hailer and hailed. It was so distanced that it breached time. It required being away from the others, any others, a good way.

Then, they could have lowered the price of their precious workout rates.

Workouts followed for Zong and some of the others. The workout trunks, which hung toward the end of the benches are over the end of it were hardly different. Zong and the others were in their suits and working out. They and themselves were relieved that being themselves, which was a quickly returning to the middle of the workout board, and they rested a moment next to the bicycle machines. Their workout trunks were from an on sale at a store, which was a good place to be.

They were on such a sale that they couldn't be passed up by shoppers, Mimi and Minnie, who had to have them, were in a throng of shoppers eager to get the deal. And returning to the others with a smile on their face, and workout gear, they smiled and headed to checkout. A smile that said, I work out so good, I do not need to hail the others worked.

They know it. They knew it their workout repetitions. Zong and Boozy rested from a long series of chin up-pull up repetitions, changing from chin up to pull up in the top of a repetition off and on, and then running around the track at the indoor facilities.

Boozy practiced the mile run to the tune of four minutes and quit at that.

He pounded out a drum rhythm of having conquered on the bench on the outdoor park bench by some picnic tables where some others were arm wrestling, and as waiting and waltzing as for the workout to come on strong got to him he left to the indoor workout., His mind was pacing, which was in a drum rhythm that would summon the best wave of physical bliss from working out possible, from the depths of his being, and he worked on taking a break while sitting on the bench.

Boozy was from the depths of a town somewhere around the horizon, so alive with parties that the going transportation took him to the workout arena. There he was with them to view ongoing martial arts through screen splicing, entirely near and far away at the same time. This was in the horizontal directions of its length.

It was a long wait and hey, someone had to use the workout place again.

This time, he laid back a little on the workout tools, disregarding the others and let go of his mind, which was mixing in with the salt water types. And his workout started to go into forever. They would have to be disbanded if they got the off-on working out as at the static offer of a special deal for less time.

Buzz came to up in another sit up and kicked a little pile of beach sand that was there stubbing his toe on the hard rock underneath the sand.

Then a kid came and said, "I get that rock when no one around real fast and think it's you."

He ran away being odd.

Then back at the end of the workout they came into the changing room changed quick and got out.

Boozy had been given a nice deal on an endless supply of gear by the sponsor, who made the medium sized weights. They were not cheap weights.

Relieved, he could workout as good as anyone there and he knew he was feeling sweat, which was better than anyone there most days. No one dared hail him.

Someone started to catch a workout time, he was catching a deep breath.

'Was it one of the Stoners?' he thought. 'No, it's an ex stoner' he concluded in his mind. 'That is an ex stoner', he thought.

It was nice when some of ex stoners got together to thank their hailers again. Indeed, they weren't all bad.

The semi pro was right there, recognizing this event as one in which there was no issue taken.

Hailing an ex stoner could have its consequences. These people might have problems.

One ex stoner was surprised if not stunned.

The hailer continued over weeks. He didn't want to get involved with any self defense team or self defense expert who might be a little unbalanced naturally from taking blows as well as unbalanced emotionally from being an acclaimed success in his field, a self overestimation.

The persons whose unbalanced nature had moved them to be well esteemed as a self defense expert were good.

Then one hailer was more than he expected, already the hailer was where most self defense experts sought, at least in their subconscious, which was of their collective unconscious association to self defense, which was supposedly meditationally devotional and sustained.

Plus or minus, it didn't matter. if there was no one to hail, no one would hail, no one would be hailed.

This got around. There were others who were being hailed. The ex-stoners were targeted, which was interrupting life in the process of living life.

It was again after one ex stoner, having been somewhat a gang member of a recreational drug users gang, that another hailer got wise. The other hailer was but one of a handful. The head, his hand in a fist that could be defined, besides having five fingers, it could be defined by how hard it balled up. And as a self defense element, it might even intail finger projection(s).

One look at the balled up fist told the bum that he would have to relax. One meditation on that was all it took.

He got hailed.

Hail bums is in the lingo that says a lot if not all.

Imagine a workout kook bum hailing someone for a spare change. Imagine some workout location worker, they were all a little simultaneous and withholding their breathing was part of it.

An event that the end dr. therapy party session determined, sometimes, even in the shallowest of possibilities, this was an understanding in the calmest of workout days.

There someone hailing a taxi cab. It's a two way street.

Work bums. Cab driver bums.

One hails bums regularly, declaring they are bums and there is little thought, one goes into hailing bums. Hailing bums goes on. Some go beyond just hailing.

The cab driver hailed, usually picks up the fare. Polished steel catches the driver's eye and he slams on the brakes, he stops the car and jumps out and runs.

The fare lights up a filter cigarette and pauses.

Some of those who are bums, that is hobo like bums, hail for fun, some for profit, none for trouble. It's a free country. This is the limit.

Somewhere, someone who hails the person of their friendship, they are a type who hails their friend, falters. They're walking alone, it's not a busy scenario.

These are the hail bums, they see hailing someone as a natural thing to do.

They've often hailed people on their way in life.

The hail bums are the people who thrive by hailing someone or something. It's in most all people, to hail is natural and goes on in one form or another, constantly brightening up things in life.

The bums are not bums, in the hobo sense, they are a group who hail. A hail bum is a two way possibility. They are hailed and they are hailing. The bum may be less group conscious and more on their own.

Most bums who said that they were somewhat composing the gang, admitted they were ex stoners.

There was Mimi, she came with Minnie. And almost always, wherever they had gotten together, wherever there was a party, Boozy was around.

Boozy was nicknamed Boozy, when he was there at the most recent party, by someone who was boozed out themselves and commenting on Buzz's frequently boozing out. And so he, Buzz, got used to being called Boozy. Sometimes he was called Buzz, when he wasn't losing a drinking black russian contest, he was hailed as one boozy. Nut being referred to as Boozy, when it was especially applicable, was in the morning of his adult life, well after he had drank in the night for several nights in a row, night after night, week after week, growing up before the drinking age had been raised three years. Which was strange because he was under a doctor's care and he had an endless supply of medicinal marijuana.

Then, he responded in an unexplainable manner. He actually liked it and yet acted different.

Sometimes he was so hungover without particularly, recently being intoxicated he considered it might be mental with himself. Maybe.

Sometimes Buzz would be there and everyone would get off on quizzing him about something he was doing. Then it was Boozy who was usually around. Boozy, it got to be.

And with feedback from some of the other ex-stoners, who were somewhat intermittent in making appearances, he was comfortable. And yet to mention, since they did appear rarely, those with anything other than a solo standing were, when they hailed from shadows and managed to be included, the inclusive type who were also illusive.

They weren't necessarily bums, but hailing someone seemed a sort of a bum task.

The task is questionably motivated. This or that hail bum might be a friend of a friend that the stoner doesn't know or remember. They might be a lonely sort on their own, able to afford to come around somewhere often enough to be familiar with someone and then hail them from the side as they go on their way.

"Huh?" Bonozy said softly after a hail bum clearly had said something.

"Hey, you." They said it again.

Bonozy knew Boozy, Mimi and Minnie, who went quickly on her way when hailed.

Boozy, when hailed was aloof as he glanced at the person and they reminded him of someone they clearly couldn't be, so they weren't that person.

Do the hail bums have a name(s)? They do.

Thought was acceptably a criteria for newsworthiness. Hailing was of thoughts.

Thought in hailing was open. The hailing could lead one to a staggered mental condition, especially if this was a hailing in which a piece of time would be taken. It could lead to a more dramatic, serious inner mind stumble. For example, where psychosis is a thought, delusion is a thought condition.

The news of such thinking situations as these were regarding social standings and could be metaphorically excused. Someone surprised Boozy once. They had hailed him from a car that sped on. But they blurred into time going by.

It was like music. The music bum in people started in family, went church, and overstated in gang. The single singer it was. The song bum singer bum was touted.

One winter was early, but most people felt it was normal. That year the music excelled, nonetheless seeming to lose air time against rapping talk radio. And by the end of the decade they had lost the battle. Eventually somewhat buried, music became hard to find as it once had been on the AM radio.

"FM radio, having been invented by a heartbreak suicide, is some foolhardy experience." said Boozy in reply to the sky after the car he was in, which had a CD and radio, was long gone. "I don't care if the wave definition is more healthy mentally. I would wonder!"

Mimi commented, "That's not necessarily a factor in the use of radio."

Mimi and Boozy decided to take it easy by inhaling deeply of the air, so full of these radio and other waves, which wouldn't be there if these waves hadn't been invented.

The stoners, who made it hard to get into a song, were possibly phantoms of someone's mind.

There was a one half memory in some people, they had it in for whichever one could relive a memory as a psychosis flashback. And if they wanted, and that would be an experience of the past, they could turn out looking better than the stoner. The fact daunted some, if not many, who would consider getting smashed. Some stoners were looking pretty good.

Some revelation of a stoner could be supported by some safe passage presumed assumed for those who hailed, they delved into such things as most familiar books, most familiar books of the book catalog could provide a means to reliving some such past experience.

And some of the crew, a small gang who were of a smaller gang, a very small gang whose members envisioned taking a break, took a break. That break, which was taking one on to an in and into being in a rock band attitude, was actually allusive.

A succumbing to like a television story of someone, anyone, who was hailed was the story for that day.

Boozy looked forward to being hailed. He headed to the place where he liked to hang out and sometimes workout.

'Like just workout for a day" said this semi pro athlete friend of his, who had reinforced him.

This winner take all contest, where the announcer stands with a stack of twenty dollar bills and hands them out one at a time to the people who come up with a means to go where the stands are, which was with glitter. The greater the effort the greater the next time of sprint win or lose. This was ok with Boozy. He had hundred dollar bills from being the who did a maneuver and came onto an overhead light brightening just then. And with a thousand dollar bill for overcoming to get there through the overhead light wave. It was a merciful way out of one therapy session and into a party.

The for the radio and television program, a coverage, which lurked in the memory of some of the very small gang member's minds, was thought to hail it for a a day, which was considered astounding.

'Hail Boozy', thought Leo.

Leo was no bum. He thought most observers at the work parties that were so helpful to the purse. Boozy went to a work crew and was hailed as overzealous, a little like a cab fare, who when having hailed the cab for a ride, their magic force attitude concluded it was a bum rap. The bum rap escape all debt did a bum deal, and besides, right is clearly containing the punch.

"After hailing a ride, he would free all his countrymen, that's how nuts he was." declared Boozy.

The work site was not allowing much in the way of free flying poles.

Two times of the same light wavering appeared to be stimulating a hailing response in each of the other simultaneously present people.

The lucky result was the cooperation of the light wave, which took one one away from full consciousness and allowed the other consciousness to set in despite the other participant.

Three

And they lingered in a successful in life friendship in the very small gang, whose large house near the road was extensively allowing lurking on its porch steps so when no one else was there the other could be unaware of that one.

The stoner person, who rented, was out and staying there was okay. Sleeping on the pillow strewn, living room floor worked and resulted of a sometimes somewhat abandoned living room and watching the television to a transpired to the end of the show with realization no one else was there attitude.

Remainders of a party that lasted overnight were few. Most survivors of a drinking contest, who had gone home at a reasonable hour, went to some homely den, where likely a vacant sofa beckoned, or a vacated room, either of which sufficed for one who had just gotten a new job. Some people, who were mentally surviving or part mentally surviving from the past going on many such ordeals such as that party, which paid off, got to try and maintain jobs.

Yet, there may have been a score of ex stoners who worked and wound up in group therapy. This was usually a client centered therapy, a classification of therapy where the client should have communication comfort, often as by a Doctor Rodgers.

Doctor Rodgers was defensive. Dr. Portini would sit in for him.

He said, "But if they could turn off the ongoing event from happening, such controlling as of the cascading mental effect from a surprise hail, the quiet type who were immediately were affected by the hail had ignored, they'd be okay."

if they wanted, the client's doctor, who could, but usually didn't abide with the thought that there are such things, it would be fatalistic.

Boozy was nozy, he pried if he felt like it. If it was into one's personal life, investigating and being aloof about it was okay.

Boozy, who lied, when he was one of the very small gang, was trustworthy, was innocent.

He had finally surprised people by being there at the group therapy, straight from a party where he had not been so straight. This had his stealth in coming and going such that it was appreciable.

Especially noted by the pseudo martial artist trainer P'zone. P'zone, who cartwheeled once in safe proximity on the pristine lawn outside the party house, once or twice before entering, was still physically cool, not worked up or huffy-puffy.

P'zone came, talked and was aloof. Boozy was inside, noting the entrance and staying aloof.

P'zone said, "I am going to the location of a group therapy."

P'zone was going to entrance the party like usual.

She also had showed up at a bank entrance.

Boozy was there and he was with some guy who looked like Leo Miveron, the celebrity.

And he, Boozy was with another person, who was an ex stoner.

'Perhaps Logan, Leo's brother, was really related to Leo. thought Boozy.

Logan, the other person, who was with the Leo Miveron, was with him and said something to Boozy.

Boozy had heard that perhaps they were friends.

He seemed never to have hailed but often heard a hail.

It was evening and the semi rural setting was subject to sounds. A few sharp cracks were echoed by a just as loud thud.

Leo said, "Nerve wracking gunshots, but too close."

P'zone, not too near Leo, overheard his comment, looked upward a little bit over the people's heads, and replied so softly he might have been talking to himself.

He said, "I was in need of a little food and I had gone for a walk, so I had hoped for this time here."

Leo commented with a drawl "What?"

The gunshots had been in the distance in the direction of the bank.

Crazy P'zone blushed, took a sip from his just received ice water and commented.

He said, "I judiciously enjoy a drink."

Leo Miveron was right there. He said, "I thought."

And then he stopped. People were looking, not particularly at any one. Some more gunshots were heard.

Leo looked super paused and thought, are those from the same gun? Are those a small, medium or large, like a forty-five, gun?

The doctor, who often looked at his group, Boozy, Mimi, and ex stoner Doug, was there, thought Leo might know for sure if those were gunshots or something else. Maybe some sort of construction going on.

Mimi was comfortable, and she spoke.

She said, "But as my new subconscious, thank you doctor for that new subconscious thing last week, it prevented me from this thought, 'the client of a group therapy who went into deciding what they were talking about was mistaken about something'. Thank you doctor. What prevented him was from accepting it as reality was possibly real was right on at the time."

The group therapy got together with Leo, Logan (his brother), P'zone, Boozy, Mimi and Minnie.

The doctor said, "Come now. Meet Leo Miveron and be with me."

He had practically drooled hungrily when she had returned with the pizza and they started eating it and some fruit.

Mini commented, "All in all, after the mornings events, I don't know where I'd go if he'd said get out. He said it was okay."

The client could always look to the other clients, but mistaking one doctor conducting the session for another who was summarily attending put the client who was in a usual enjoyment state of mind, up for most of what most of the clients were gulping down in the way of therapeutic things the doctor said."

The doctor was a good hypnotist, though that was not his professed area.

Mimi said, "Doctor."

It was time for Mimi to talk and she hesitated.

Dr. Daler was right there to the rescue.

He said, "Yes, go on."

Mimi went on to almost ruminating, 'I had been completely nerve wracked by noon and if it was not turning out to be a nice, calm, easy afternoon."

Boozy, Mimi and Bonozy were in the group. And nobody was starting to describe how much he/she liked living there in the basement. They had all heard about Zong.

Bonozy said, "There were times a friend from in the basement where I lived came to a group therapy session and times when he did not. Ugg is like that. I didn't know Zong."

"Ugg would have liked the last of the series of the group therapy sessions." said Mimi. "But that Young guy, I don't know."

Boozy added, "Because there is fresh coffee at the dining room table along with pieces of cakes, pastries and condiments for the coffee, which are all organic, I will be sane and stay out of the picture."

Mimi replied, "And since Ugg likes these things, we can expect him to show up. He'll probably be late. Maybe he's in the waiting room having coffee right now."

"Ya, I like Doug to get my coffee." said Mimi.

The first party, second introduction to Leo, group therapy.

As pseudo psychedelicized cats watched a kaleidoscopic display in a movie theater, which was with very little music, the home party would get established.

Mimi had been a cab driver for a few years and had declared one of her memories as a cab driver over the edge. A Dr. Portini had called for a cab and she got the fare. It was a long ride and so it paid off well.

Dr. Portini, who took over temporarily for Dr. Rodgers, was a noted psychologist who specialized in group therapy for ex-stoners who were going to a party.

Mimi had invited him to her house party at Ridge Rd. where she owned the house. It was a new records party and would be happening again in two months.

Boozy said, "Ya, I knew it was likely he'd be over the edge."

Mimi commented, "If there was another cab driver, who was declaring that they were on the tan escalator, then we'd be on flying saucers."

This was the next generation of *flying saucer* to hit the streets after sunshine. This was the thought anyway.

Work could proceed, maybe a cab driver was on it? And since there were many a job to do many people like Boozy, who ably worked and Bonzy, who had a job, worked.

Mimi picked up some passengers, who sometimes were ailing, and some fare who was drunk bought her a drink, dragging her against her shyness, coaxing, into a pub, which allowed the concentration of customers to cancel the experience enough to do the job. There was a side moment then, which was a norm for cab drivers, a wait for a call to this or that fare, and this side moment took Mimi out of the cab to a head shop with music. And to the side, which was enjoyed in the idea of having a good time, other patrons showed what a good time the *escalator* could be.

Mimi said, "I drove on, the taxi was a good car."

There was the fiasco half a ten on a beef call, a hail of a type.

There was what took a saucer to look at for a six hour venture

And another cab this one time took workers to a site, took to taking groups of men to an unloading of a container of chairs. What happened, which was going on in such a hustle, it was like a scene from a comedy movie. If there was an acting class on, it would have been with a laugh.

Chairs usually stack up nicely. Brand new chairs stacked like scoops of ice cream in a ice cream shop were slid across a half empty container to the pallette where they'd be laid sideways, as the forklift flew into position and whipped around to set the palette down once it was full, chairs were being stacked, and another empty palette was soon put in place for more chairs.

Leo walked by the site in the afternoon a few days later while the foreman's nerves were still getting together. A mischievous mood had Leo, he had been drinking to the max, and as he passed the workers getting off, who were just getting off and going in the opposite direction in the back of a pickup truck, he made a hand wave that looked ominous.

Leo's long lost brother, who had just happened to be around, came around the corner and was soon with Leo. Leo stood there for a moment and saw Boozy, who was walking it from a nearby job. Boozy walked to the other side of the street feeling a little like the lonely guy he sometimes was and passed in front of them.

Leo said, "Hey, Boozer."

Boozy said, "Boozy."

When it was over and this Leo was nowhere around, he talked to a policeman, who was waking him up.

Boozy said, "People were strange. Other guys see eyes, this guys eyes seemed to peer at me from behind a plate glass window. Like those over there. And here."

There were some offices of the work sites nearby that had nice, large plate glass windows. There was some broken bits of glass nearby.

Leo was thinking as he walked around the block and away, 'from the beginning of this day, it's been one of those days when I had been thinking of going somewhere, and the wind was at me, out to get me as I had been minding my business. I go where I go.'

He said out loud, "I got to get off the meds."

Leo's brother might have been long gone and Leo may have been lost but the brothers they were went this way and without much time they had a reunification.

His brother, who was infrequently around, Logan, reported he was with a friend, a girlfriend. She wasn't right there.

Logan said, "And I'm turning my girlfriend on for the drive in show tonight.

"Later, with a case of beer and a friend with a boat, we're on a cruise sometime. Some enjoyment with a pot toke is there, too."

"A pot toke." Leo echoed.

Nonetheless, these get-togethers happened regularly and frequently. Leo and *Logan* went their ways for the time being.

The client centered therapy could have a turn of events. It might become doctor, or therapist, centered therapy. Mimi thought if that happened it would be more fearful.

Doctor Portini was in charge of his clients. The sat comfortable. At this one place, it was a meal included. The one get-together, Boozy and Mimi conversed, worked out real good. It was there and they responded to a nonverbal cue from the doctor, a nod.

Mimi commented, "A tiny psychout of the dusty room with granules to sweep up. It relaxed me real good tool Relax you too."

"What do you mean, relaxed?" quizzed Dr. Portini.

"Long after having my last, pronounced by a friend post last time, such an experience time went off like a change in the weather." said Boozy.

"What do you mean pronounced, Boozy? You boozing?"

"The thing was, a friend, who was murdered, had said, 'when you know it, you take your last hit of' and he trailed off."

"I dug the pronouncement thinking through many a trips to feel good, is this the last time. I had a last time. But then this pay off thing, a little different. The payoff was so okay. Years later, I just tasted the small five hundred or so miles of highway. But it was over in a few weeks. The pronouncement, which I respected, had a stay after that. Not because I was paranoid or anything, not just because I respected the person."

Mimi answered, "You know, Boozy, that isn't much of a get you high pay the rent event."

"That's right, Mimi." answered Boozy. "But so what?"

Mimi was right there with him. She asked, "You enjoyed that?"

Boozy commented, "Sure did. Took me right to an enjoyable sleep.

"There were driving through trips, and a wrecked car time was way back. I was getting into a trying of the simulations."

"There was a wrecked time way back." said Mimi. "Someone left it in a friend's yard. They said they heard someone talking outside, but no one was there."

A number of them, who were trying to get somewhere were of the the theatre there, which was a day on the mainland and flute playing at the park till the sun went down, and a morning after in the city.

"There we was an on the streets of on with a guitar at a small park.

There was a dear feast from with musicians in a country rock house.

There were from near there and the number of them trying those who knew where it was at in at party, it was with drinking.

There was intensity living near on some kind of a day. So we got to where we was having a nightly ride on horseback, which was off to the dawn.

Someone, so totalled was with a jew's harp, blues band playing all morning onto late coming to work, and it was a trip driving with friends. There was following them in his car, down to the strip where slowing of a cruising and the flashing lights occurred.

"I could remember all those trips of several years back and look at them now like then, they were well spaced out trips." Boozy said.

It took some years, it seemed as well, remembering other times to have made a complete expression of such times.

But making a clinical like study of the experiences fades.

Boozy said, "Although there may be some value in perusing that in the realm of thought, it would take more nerve than I could muster."

But for the most part, it was this account of trips to provide a list of times of a past and interesting part of life, when one is middle-aged, taking a last trip and decided to take no more, it goes to remembering, in one form of the flash back as a time that may have occurred. One was to find many years later conclusions the trip was actually on occasion extremely small amounts, or use produced immunity.

But I was a welfare recipient at some points sin time of from then on and fortunately one could right and be something else besides that. Which had been doing, spending some of ones dimes doing? Lo and behold, one is off welfare and government programs for education loans.

"The point is," Bonozy said, "that in the morning up and at 'em, one is at a point in time that starts in class y around the clock waking up as usual, going to coffee, and the combing the hair routine.

One first impress of life as a dormitory called home goes to automatically being a still being writing in points in time as notes, and it's strongly windy. One notes an event and it's pretty even far windy. It is cool to. For this time of a morning its at the yet, it's not unusual for the time of year, and it is important for there to be such a thing as talk among friends. And family is about the changing weather which is so reassuring that thought is to reminisce about reassurance that it was a weather of years about some before that particularly windy eyar, its strength as coolness sets in.

"Yet this is like considering of the question of the weather." Minnie commented.

Mimi replied, "It's that strong of a wind, it was generally a new and familiar air, it was at a point in time when the water everywhere was so good to drink."

"It's so heavy," Boozy said. "Drinkers drinking there are too, are mostly going along with it and getting stoned."

One was into getting stoned before playing on in life, somewhat of an experimental self life basis when actually, getting stoned got heavy. One would be exactly out of order if what they took was the of the list of those most times that they remembered was taking them into a state of being in which bounding ar the party that needed more beer.

Let one start by attempting to explore a detail. One of the many drk experiences available to someone's mind came through the memory. Boozy explained this drinking experiences and its drug relationship were nowhere close to the others special bum outs he was having,

Mimi owned a car which had been given to her. It was the only car of which about a dozen vehicle shad been given to her.

She said, "The car was working out fairly well for me."

A good friend often had it available and some car's psychedelic paint jobs, which were there under the rugs.

Though this was not a big money expense, the was often given a try. Although one was not likely to have effect in any hallucinogenic way, it seemed unfair there was an undertaking to do so when it wasn't technically a boozing.

Boozy, who was in effect, said, "It's me in a way."

Then it wasn't so one friend or another would probably obtain most any drug one knew about.

Boozy and Mimi were able to take it occasionally.

A usual, it was some other day and another way to get a good view of a psychedelic art done up on a hospital wall. It was like a drug, i.e., medicinal, which took us to work. And it sort of took them over the past, to the phase when it was dry. Boozy would take and get.

He said, "Smoking my own roll jobs was my life in an recognized state of money"

He was at least a standard ex stoner retrying it for the rule, and he saw the residence of it, he was where he was at as an event and on weekend parties. Some such residents were with him on that, though they were just experimenting with it.

"I experimented with." said Boozy,

"With none. You came up big for the go straight." said Mimi.

Residents of the area's ex stoner group were comfortable in parlours, cottages and outings where temporary shelters included camper vehicles and tents where there were stakes in the ground, and tents which had few stakes and fancy appurtenances to keep them up. Some were quite homey, large and had poles.

The breeze wafted into an ex stoner's nostrils carrying numerous elements of the catalogue of peaceful times. At times the normal barrage of the many categories of right on presences affected Boozy. The airs that from a nearby at that place auto work site were rarely outdone by regular outside airs of second hand from stoners in cars passing bus stops where ex stoners sat waiting was notable and sidewalks where ex stoners roam had some sort of trash by them at times.

The ex stoners, who were having a party, were quite lucky that there were many a very small gang to show up. Besides these newcomers were the non ex stoners, pseudo ex stoners. Nothing wrong with them. Actually they were in the groove of the many parties going on.

One ex stoner, Mimi and another, Boozy, supposed to be an ex stoner, were at the party, which was up to strength with characters like Boozy and at times the party was raging with conversation overriding the music, which was boombox level, sometimes a radio channel. Some twenty regular party goers more or less owned the party, talking was incessant, regardless of it was at a small cottage where lived someone.

Someone lived by the very small, ex-stoner gang's cottage. Another such very small gang to show up would have been disruptive.

"Turn that thing down." someone said.

Boozy, who knew the whereabouts of the party because he had been there before and had recently heard there would be a repeat of it that night, came with a girlfriend, N. The girlfriend, having heard about it happening was very enthused.

In that the party was dramatic, it was open and there were a lot of people coming and going. As just another one of these, quite a few parties were being attended by a regular, very small gang there, there were parties that had little more than fifty people there, there was drama. A number of persons brought a guest, so there were additional people. A person brought a sample from their dinners, and another person brought a radio, another person brought another radio. One of the people was there as a guest of honor. There were numerous guests of honor at the party.

Another party was a carbon copy of the ongoing party. People liked the companionship of the party, they liked their knowing friends there were with the same ilk.

The ex stoners had a party rolling. The rolling party had finally become a regular occurrence.

P'Zone came a little late for the start. He sat on the front steps, a porch like thing, while most of the party was well inside listening to records.

P'Zone was interested in impressing his friends who were putting the party on, and protecting himself should someone go beyond just hailing him and actually push him or knock the block off his shoulder should someone put one there. He couldn't balance things that well and had to rely on someone to put a block on his shoulder if anyone were stupid enough to knock it off. He sat there and ate peanuts from a bag. He liked nuts. And to add to his abilities of being able to protect himself from stupid people, besides throwing his arms around like a windmill, supposed to be in opposite directions, he decided to build up his hands.

While he had cracked many a pecan with a pecan, and eating pecans had always been something special to him, he rarely failed to crack at least one of the two pecans he placed in his palm, and squeezed. Eat more nuts was the answer as he came up with a plan, crack a brazil nut and eat it.

"I'll place the pecan on the concrete step where I am sitting and crack it with the side of my hand." He said.

One of the guests peeked out of the nearby living room doorway. An athlete, who had become acquainted with him the day before, smiled and commented.

The guy said, "Fly like a dove."

P'Zone cracked two pecans at one time and held out the pieces to his friend. Zong ate the pecan meat, hastily picking that from the many sharp, shell fragments and inner pulp.

He said, "Let's dance."

The guy said, "You can eat peanut shells, you know."

"Don't tell him that." cried the nosey host Boozy, nearby on the inside of the doorway. "He'll know anything."

P'Zone liked peanuts. His friend, the guy, told him, "Ya, there is a lot of nutrition in the shells. Elephants eat peanuts with the shells."

P'Zone replied, "Ya. And so do monkeys."

He cracked two more pecans and ate them quickly picking the meat and tossing the remains to the side of the steps.

The party was soon over, but it would come together again in three days. There and then, it was happening, and P'Zone appeared on the steps cracking a nut.

This time, he set one pecan down on the smooth cement surface next to him, stood up and suddenly, somewhat lightly, stomped on it giving off a similar crack sound as when he cracked on or two in his hand.

The guy was at the party and stuck his head out the door, looked at the little P'Zone scene, P"Zong looked at him and sat down and started picking the meat of the nut and eating it, swishing the pieces off to the side. The guy hailed him.

He said, "Hey Zong."

P'zone replied, "Zoong's okay."

Zong said, "I took your advice and ate some peanuts in the shell. They were alright."

The guy gave him some advice, "Eat shrimp tails."

Zong sat back down and said, "How is the party going."

Just then there was a new record being placed on the turntable.

Those who desired the company, had gathered at Mimi,'s house. It was someone whose open house party formula had worked. She owned the house, another house two houses away and an apartment two blocks away.

Things were pretty smooth for a while.

Maybe they watched television, ate potato chips, and engaged in parlor games, board games, or card games. These ex stoners enjoyed the ongoing event of socializing.

Boozy walked out without saying bye to anyone. He was embarrassed in his unconscious, the collective unconscious of the party goers were not supporting his embarrassment and that increased his anxiety. He was anxious when he walked out. He was a little sad. No one seemed to notice that he had left on the surface.

There inside was Mimi. She wondered, shyoy to herself, if her friend Boozy was coming right back. Boozy thought for a second on it and let it pass. He was going to come back when he was ready. Others, who had came and went away were always doing so with some link to existing and usually present parties. Someone came when someone left. Someone coming into noted mentally that Bozzy was going, going, gone. Zong went inside to use the restroom, used the restroom, ate some potato chips, was offered a cold drink (non alcoholic), he took it and sat in the one available soft seat, a big cushioned chair, relaxed and listened to the pretty loud stereo, which was just opposite to the side of his seat.

A social gathering is generally dramatic, where the people socialize, social activity is dramatic activity, such social dramatic activity is light drama. Heavy drama is merely theatre.

Tuesday was as the day after the day party event.

One of the social party experiences happened at the same house. Usually at the same time. When the party was over, it took an hour to find it vacated except for the residents.

Usually there were some outsiders, who didn't get in the door because they couldn't find a parking place for their car and didn't want to walk over half a mile to socialize. And some came any way. The event was a day in which all day could transpire. It might transpire into the night and through it.

It was soon the next day, the very small group was intensely listening to records. This was no big such party. There was a long pause, Mimi and Boozy played blackjack for fun, turning cards. Sometimes they played rummy.

Mimi broke the silence by describing an episode she had had with her medicinals.

Boozy had just come in this time, he came in just as she was about to speak, which broke into her approach for a second. Zong looked up glassy eyed from his relief of having a glass of cool, purified water he was drinking, He looked at a woozy Boozy, Boozy was woozy from walking to the group meeting, which was a one mile walk. It was after visiting one or another of a many get togethers that were going on those days.

Four

Dr. Portini, Drew Portini, was a psychologist who taught classes in physical development on the side. He could take anyone. His motto was, I am someone who loves life and nothing bothers me that I don't allow. He gave his friendship to his clients.

Bo Nozy saw Dr. Portini several times before going to one of his group sessions. The sessions usually included those people he was in acquaintance and friendships with, Mimi and Minnie the two girls, a husky guy and his brother (sometimes present), and Z. Zong and Y. Zoong his acquaintances who were followers of this Dr. Portini crowd, and a few others. Boozy was especially keen on Dr. Portini's help.

Boozy was like Buzzy another character who liked to attend parties.

Boozy talked to his friends Z. Zong and Y. Zoong and they asked him how he was doing.

As he was known as Zoong, Y. Zoong asked, "How are you doing?"

Z. Zong standing next to him said, "What's up?"

Boozy replied, "That doctor psychologist is helping me fine. Not only with therapy. But I'm into an ongoing appreciation of the work out."

"Who is the doctor?" asked Zong.

"Dr. Portini, the therapist." Boozy replied.

Dr. Portini was the psychologist. He was one of the new 'my psychologist' psychologists. He had started many a client into the college of martial arts, which went worldwide based on findings in the leading large data databases. He would help out a client from time to time, who needed a place to stay by letting them use his old truck, which was set up like a room. To the person it was a room. Nonetheless of a client's willingness to be seen, he found many clients who would be recommended to follow up therapy with a psychiatrist. And he knew quite a few psychiatrists as colleagues. A couple were quite into martial arts and protected themselves as the needs arose.

One case he usually told, by Dr. Portini, had the psychiatrist instantly block a swing from the client. The poor client, who came unglued and had let themselves break through the barrier of normalcy in human to human conversation took a swing at the interviewing psychiatrist.

"I may have needed a doctor like that." said Bo Nozy when he heard of this event from Dr. Portini in private.

Bo Nozy was known to have broke down in a violent letting go, but nobody ever proved anything on that nor took him to court. He was like Boozy, he had his regrets, and regularly saw Dr. Portini or one of his colleagues.

Bo Nozy told Dr. Portini his tale of wild gangs jumping at seeing him.

He said, "Doctor Portini, I was just minding my own business when this small group of guys, five I think, interrupted my flow of thought by disturbing my mind with their clamor. The biggest of them pulled my shoulder from behind a little, and I got kinda upset. I heavily shrugged him off. So the other two guys moved to this guys aid, I faced them and I had pushed him back with both hands at once. There was a vicious fight and I had to punch them all real quick. Fortunately they were taking it and backing off. One guy pushed over, lying down, which was because I knocked them down complained, 'you!'."

"Now, Dr. Portini, I got a problem with my need to go somewhere and my car broke down."

Doctor Portini answered, "My friend, you may borrow my car as long as you return it in two days."

Bo Nozy replied affirmatively, "Thanks Dr. Portini, I needed that."

Pody, as he had been referred to, was him, he was Pody Bo Nozy.

He thought a minute. 'Till all hours of the night sometimes, I heard voices talking and wondered where they were coming from. I heard a phone ringing from a next door neighbor'.

His old clock drove him bananas, its gears grinding away. And as his old refrigerator had kept him company, not exceptionally when it stopped to rest by annoying him with an occasional whistle, while dripping water that pooled, he nonetheless relaxed. He would clean it up. And he did clean the refrigerator especially in front where it leaked.

It seemed somebody was always building something nearby. Almost a boom town racket!

Across the road from where he lived, a narrow two lane blacktop from his house, a pool game held court. Sometimes late in the evening he heard it, sharpening his hearing, the ball breaks. As a distant disco partying was going on, it's bass was heard from that far away.

A gun was fired rarely. But if so, between the disco and where the pool ball broke. A lone flute soft and sullen, beautifully was played in the after midnight hours on nearly rare nights.

It may have happened from the first days of Bo Nozy's life there. He thought, 'I don't know, may have happened to Boozy, too. Some guys gave him trouble.'

Dr. Portini's comment stayed with him, 'I have only thought it possibly so'.

Then it would get really quiet. His phone rang and he answered it. Was it his old friend, Leo Mivrin? He wondered. Leo was smart, he had asked him if there were any spare rooms or secretive types in his neighborhood.

Leo had said on the phone, "Would people like a programming for the public citizen to go secret, where they're all secret agents?" and then, "I'm coming over."

Leo had his foibles. And since he was an old friend and could, would and did pay some of the rent after he was welcome to share and stay, Leo the acquaintance lingered on. He was often leaving for a while and coming back. 'Was he across the street?' wondered Poby Bo Nozy.

And the acquaintance friend slowly moved out and moved on to where? He wouldn't say. Just there was a place.

Bo Nozy had his house by a narrow road. A small house. The road a well used lane.

The days turned to months. Bo Nozy thought, 'night after night, my feeling is to just keep quiet and to keep an eye open for this friend'. Little did he know it but his friend Leo kept an eye open when he slept. He noticed it once when his friend, sleeping in his living room, actually had one eye about half open. He kept an eye open. Too bad if he moved on thought Bo Nozy.

But if the explanation was given to him, which would explain this or that event, suggested the event had support of credibility since it was made up and was a falsity were true, there was a secondary thought. Bo Nozy thought and thought, 'the make up for one being the host and being secretive and agent like secretiveness could be from a agency of some persons, parents probably, maybe relatives orientation, which could be what he was talking about'. He considered!

Then, Boozy came. Boozy was adjusted to normalcy in life. Around his nineteenth age he stepped up, he went to maybe have some super meal, which were beneficial and also found supporting by his friend. They were in a food and milk diet.

The generous cats, his friends, who brought it in had bought it.

Boozy was the tenant of this place quite like Pony Bo Nozy. Boozy, however, took out his frustrations with justification. He was supported in his taking out his frustrations by a therapy that did just that. He watched, first, on his TV the practitioners of berzerk destruction demolishing well used cars, which somebody had to clean up, with sledge hammers and heavy construction (manual) equipment. This was a secure event. The next step he saw a coordinated businesses and municipal permits allowing it, lots were to be totaled.

He little thought how much it would cost him to replace such and such an item. He shivered himself back to normalcy.

For the most part Boozy took walks. He was limited to places nearby.

He spent time on the telephone, his caller would call again.

He called a suicidal center hotline for someone to talk to, again and again, week after week and also, the next month and years later. He was interested in that career, telephone answerer.

Then, some cats were secretive themselves, even though they threw up in the gutter from having drank too much and it was possible that they had their drinks given them. It was with some such anti people-collision affect, that they would have the throw up. And they themselves claimed they had had to jump from a moving car window to escape the heat programmers.

But this was not the case for Poby Bo Nozy. He was not one of those people, he was not a strange cat.

It was part of the expose response on a questionnaire and he would not even dare to jump out of a moving car much less a car window.

Bo Nozy later said, "That's freaky."

The cat had called and complained about his other friends.

The cat said, "They bombarded us with some kind of lecture, man. It's some frizz result on me when I's at an earlier age, I supposedly was worked on, lecture to being developed up to it. This was until when later I had a room, Was at my room in a house where I lived and they that brought out the scene, was so they likely to get me accosted."

One of the group Yesterday People, a long haired guy from the next neighborhood, came and said, "He has my schizophrenia!"

Boozy looked had around and then at Poby Bo Nozy.

Poby cautiously answered at the front door. He turned around when the caller left.

He said, "He usually provided me a meal and I was in such need. But his sounds kinda bothered me. No one wise cracks at three in the morning."

It had really become stronger, the problem, over the course of years. Bo Nozy and Boozy went separately to doctors. There was an interim doctor who saw them both, along with some girls from their neighborhood. The occasion of a waiting room session came when they had to wait on the doctor.

"No, I don't think so." said the doctor.

"So, no, it's not while I am there that this may still be happening?" Boozy asked, retorting.

The doctor was frank, "No, do some antipsychotic thinking? Not so okay. Then supposing it's someone who is talking to you. It hasn't panned out yet has it?"

Boozy looked at the banana peel in the old window sill above his kitchen sink. It had been there four days and was starting to become well dried. The next time ne looked it had turned black.

It was days later and he crumbled the peels up and put it on his stove top, turned the stove on, and watched the thin fume rise in the air. He had to breathe and he did breathe in.

It was a dry time for Boozy, dry from the medicinal marijuana he was normally finding access to with his permit, dry from the even the mild herbal tea concoction that had run out, he used it for a time up to a few weeks to assuage his desire for his regular medicinal. The dried banana peel was like that.

Some success came for Boozy with head butting a thin board to crack it. Then, rather than resorting to cripping blows to break it, he thought don't. And he didn't.

Aside from his kitchen, his thoughts built up on how to defend himself should such an event as that needing defensive action came up, which he kept aloof from, mentally and such an event never happened.

Subsequently with acquaintances into a college of self defensive martial arts, an acquaintance was the expert, lectured his friend.

He said, "You got crazy mixed up. When I didn't get mixed up, and I found myself face to face with a real hot practitioner of a martial arts the thing went ballistic I got crazy mixed up. You get crazy mixed up."

This wound up as the mix up to further el aZ

Exasperated by Boozy, Leo had a fit, his jealousy based unknown martial arts mix up including sport consideration was to blame, and since he, nevertheless of the nuttiness of this, continued to lecture, he was put on temporary leave and threatened with a restraining order. He thought, 'they better go visit his friend who lived in a tropical climate. Where the bananas grew'.

He went. He would return.

When he got there his friend welcomed him with open arms.

Atlas, his friend said, "The mastery in action is dwelling, so go with the flow and keep taking the in-place paces at double time."

Leo Mivrin replied, "I think I'll take a look at your little bit ol banana patch. OK?"

The three clumps of banana trees grew close together on the edge of a garden, which was about a half mile from his friend's house. His friend Atlas, who knew Zong, accompanied him to it. He was standing arms crossed on his chest, they were enjoying the fresh air, and suddenly Atlas let his right hand fly and it landed squarely on the adjacent, large, bearing fruit (small, green) banana tree trunk, indenting its material compressed about three-quarter inch. The tree sap slightly appeared from the smooth surface of the trunk being broken into.

Atlas then struck it similarly to the hand fly but with a more balled fist, only now he let his fist ricochet onto the adjacent banana tree in that clump, there were five trees, one having just grown high enough to be be punched back like that without faltering, having recently given fruit and

Atlas, the caretaker, had used his machete to chop it, with one fell swing at its base, standard banana tree treatment for the upcoming tree, right out of the stalk center would become the new tree. Atlas glanced another fist strike, and used his elbow on the next adjacent tree while kneeing the third tree, similarly not too hard so as not to hurt his knee.

Atlas said, "Watch this."

He then took about five paces back, pulled a knife with an about six inch blade and a broken wood handle, tossed it and caught the blade ever so lightly and rightly, rightly with the blace sharp side out and balanced for a perfect throw. He cocked his arm a bit and threw the knife to the third tree, where after one and a half turns in flight, it stuck fairly deep in the banana tree trunk, causing more of the banana sap to come out; and he chased it with a quick walk to the trees, stuck quickly his right elbow, punching it therein, the adjacent tree, glanced a punch from the first tree back into the same tree and kicked the fourth tree of the clump with the ball of his foot, in glancing he sped up his pace of delivery of punches and in an instant was relaxing looking at this visiting Leo.

"Then at each pace," he lectured at the college, "I revolved around in equal practice repetitions at the same place and strove to double time a double timed event of it again. This in one occasion, supplied a brief moment of flight levitation, which would be assumed pure escape in the event of need be. Even if it was fudging off reality a bit. I did it.

"In the event of losing your temper," said Atlas Zong, one of the right handed specialists from overseas, a player in the background at the college, "it come to life. And I have to tell you, this finds its target."

Why wasn't anyone interested in hearing about this? They had little to do with a close person, who many years earlier before was with those who were into it. They were born into it, so they had envy from others. It was recommended to arm swing like a windmill.

"I went like a windmill. Then I calmed down and became obsessed with cracking nuts with my hands." said Zoong at the college. "It started with little pecans, then walnuts, then thick shelled pecans. They were nuts to try and crack that brazil nut."

Then they used walnuts and would hit them with a hard, well-directed as having point direction to their object, a part of their hand doing it was in mind. The nut was on a nice, brick pedestal."

Zoong could have broke the brick he was so freaked out.

He ate the nuts he cracked, picking them with his finger tips, continuously for two years. Working up to include brazil nuts, which required deciding a place to put the attention, he was wielding his right palm with a rather calloused side.

Boozy's forehead, which eventually came to have a nerve aberration thing, in later years, would work its way up to near his spine and become a problem. This was found by a physician to have resulted of the nut crack attempts. He became considered used, similarly. Only getting angry would wake up the calouse as it was being directed.

This person, Boozy thought, this was with so many years later, he would take up the Kup school, double lessons on his own, despite his becoming a little suspicious. Boozy took up the art and he was soon drop kicking static, soft objects, with one consideration for shortcomings in double drop kicking the pillows, which were there, as this was possible. He tossed another one up and landed both feet in it and came down on his feet.

He was ready for some double time empty air push punch exercise, which he did. The result increased his escape flight mechanism.

"Once I had bought a quart of beer and drank it." Boozy said. "I ducked the stares of onlookers from other cars in the parking lot. Punched a parked car fender harmlessly! They were not there to me, though from the corner of my eye it seemed someone was looking. I came to full wakefulness commenting to the companion fender, which was in vain."

He needed a doctor. And replied to the doctor.

Boozy said, "I became intoxicated, it ruined my life. So I attend a party for non drinkers. That's why I'm here."

Bertrand, Bo Nozy's friend, who was called Bo Nozy's friend by his friends was sometimes there, sometimes not and had opinions on these things.

Boozy was doing the exercise in his rooming house room.

There was at a regular meeting of ex stoners under the leadership of Dr. Portini, who specialized in groups of ex stoners. There was frank discussion. A less formal party often occurred, much through the graciousness of the hosts. Mimi and Minnie were young ladies often having a major party and sometimes the party just happened with their consent.

The doctor's office was busy.

"It was you was a light drinker?" asked Zong.

Dr. Portini replied, "I don't drink, Zong. If I were you, I wouldn't drink."

The party was on. It was one of several non intoxication gatherings. Boozy, the hosts and the others were sitting in a semicircle.

Mimi said, "I painted my art on the bare floor, this was with paint I got at a hardware store. So abuse in the fumes is not an element for consideration. That's what most professional house, room, painters say. Anyway, it's long time dry."

The room's floor, which was basically smooth concrete, was dotted with blue and brown enamel.

Mimi went on, "I added candy apple red from a spray paint and stenciled it with movie film for consecutive dots, of purple of my now canvas like work of a floor."

She paused and went on, "These inspirations were leftovers from a special effects fantasy I was into with some friends at their large house's living room. For a while my fantasies were okay, they were played out. Recently, I put this paint on and within a day slept on it."

Boozy and Bo Nozy looked around themselves and admired the fantastic art. The ex stoner party thing was taking precedence.

Boozy commented, "I soon returned to my same old place. It was then with the fate of drug store drug and alcohol taking, a long, hard road of self rehabilitation, which was guided by counseling sessions from Dr. Portini, who was inclined to donate his two cents as I went into detox time and time again"

Zoong was next, he said, "I smoked a little weed and we went on a hike. Then, this friend of mine, who was with his wife and sometimes was on his own, came to my next personal outing to the countryside ambience. I don't know what they were doing out there, but they came back in no time looking a bit relaxed."

The doctor said, "Nosiness has its problems. So I don't get too nosy. But with drugs, it was an escape. I was once also getting away from the clutches of a drug addiction habit and instead of adapting to the patterns of most people who work, taking drugs locked me into seeing things from the exterior, which I applied to my philosophizing, I studied and became a doctor."

The doctor's sessions came and went and came again. In between was a party.

Mimi, acting as the moderator at the party said, "So you were a doctor taking drugs, a philosopher who took drugs?"

Doctor Portini, who occasionally came to these parties, was caught off guard in thought and the others were quiet allowing him to recompose, as was their experience also.

Next to the talker was Logan, a professional student visiting his brother Leo in the area. He was well in his thirties. His dorm room, which was sustaining being littered, was littered with three empty bottles of hard liquor, old, dirty clothes and an unmade bed with the mattress showing, the sheets scrunched up with a pillow so he could read in bed. He still kept up with his studies. This was a party expounding and Dr. Portini enjoyed it.

Logan said, "In my second dormitory room, which was not too close to the first one opposite a resident manager's apartment, me and my personality had thought that through the years of schooling, I would get professional. I thought, 'this is not hitchhiking or drug taking'. But after surprise, simple medicinal drug use habit developed and followed me wherever I went, I quit for good."

The next person was Abby. Abby was a newcomer, he had a lot to say and only a little while to say it.

Abby said, "I was a young man and wanted to mate to the female I liked from a fifth world family to produce a special family heritage. I thought and thought! Then they were okay with me and it broke their heart to we got together with them on my ways."

Then there was a possible third person involvement. Everyone looked. Abby was from a melting pot city.

Abby went on, "The infant, who had supposedly been an Alzheimer's neuronal cell donor, was grown up wondering! This is what he found. The person her infant son donated to was of the other world. And years earlier, they had been given an Alzheimer's neural cell donor treatment, and they were doing so fine it was recommended to others to get such a treatment. And so I signed a willing to donate form for any upcoming children, in that event of special possibilities that if it came up for my infant child, it meant it came up and that would allow it with my blessings."

Dr. Portini answered, "That's nice. I was aware of these kinds of events and so was with the authorities of our concern. Happens a lot?"

But this was only the tip of the iceberg. It did work out. Now the group session was from the doctor's office.

Boozy started blurting out, "Me, in my third year was next. I was nearly fifty three and had skull invasive operation, similar in which the brain was nearly temporarily exposed. There would be blood. Then, for the where the brain fragments of intelligence were thought peopled-in, I could connect."

Dr. Portini informed the party further, "Sometimes in the later years, those donors are responsible and so are taken to signing release forms so that after their death, these were authors, scientists, even elected officials, that soon after they were dead, their neural specific could be laced into a donor brain at the site where the Alzheimer's donation was from. You are informed and asked to sign before the skull part was put back. About the size of a quarter was put back in."

Boozy added, "I was assuming this was alright, these were special and these signed release, no longer secret advances in these sciences that allowed this development, had form releases, which were a special project of the head of it happening. So! And we are finding out it was true."

Bo Nozy also blurted out, "As the things grew, and I grew up as my somewhat secluded scars completely healed over, the graft was a success and the outer skin regenerated. This was supposedly what the secret of age extension and could be attributed to the health of donors."

Getting permission forms signed, as agents Tagas and Sincehe of the agency that oversaw this and who were on the other side, was possible. Convincing people was with unapproved display of mixed up crazy martial art.

The doctor sought to acknowledge some usually pretty easy with the generous cash payments being made efforts. And this was mostly like of incorrectly assuming there were other donors and recipients who were exposed to other so called donors and recipients about in the area. Most of them grew up to be practitioners of a mixed up crazy martial art.

"I lived nearby where this was happening." said Boozy. "This was where I came in with responses so slight not even being uncomfortable events happened. And I was being non delusional on purpose. It wasn't easy."

There were operations, with sharp objects and preparations to the body, usually on that side of the head that is subject to say the least to expression. So they found out there were some others who were assuming they were into having been on the other side.

This discussion continued at the doctor's office.

Minnie added, "And with us, who were continuing retaliation against the area where we lived for doing this, which was against our policy, there was a lot of forgetting."

"So I gave up drinking." said Boozy. "One more dream like that and I decided which pill to take was best. So when I was taking medications, I could avoid crazy mixed up martial art antianxiety and use over the counter antidepressants and other over the counter meds."

"And I just think it's better."

"Which one is most important?" asked Doctor Portini, the group's conducting head. "Antidepressants or other meds?"

Boozy answered, "Other meds. Going on, I would eventually drift back to sleep and take the supplement pills."

And outside the cigar's butts were on the side of the street, which placed Boozy in an enthusiastic state of getting some cigars, but not right then.

He went on, "They beckoned me to pick them up. I eventually picked a good one up and mentioned this to girl I met, and she stayed with me on my sofa in the living room for a week."

Then, after the doctor said this was going good, it came back to Logan.

Logan said, "This came to time to get pick up rides from family and friends, who were going to the store or bus stop. When it finally happened. I met Zong and Zoong."

They all were habitually staying up late drinking coffee. A line formed at the table with the coffee and donuts. Zong, who had gone to one of the nearby concerts recently and he was still buzzing, sat solitary way up from the bakery goods and enjoyed the music. Outside, Zoong smoked a cigar. He tossed the butt and went back inside. The meeting was adjourned and everyone went home, the doctor last.

Abby answered the door where he lived and had shared some of his thoughts with the group on wandering mothers and expressed his concern on the matter, stressing the need for care there. Who would have let their kids be involved in this? He would have given them chocolates and noted, if applicable, these kids are screamers.

Abby, who took medications from way back, said things.

He said, "Most of this other problem were from some time later, which showed in this schizophrenia."

After he got back from a counseling session, he relaxed on a floor mat at Boozy's home for a while. Before, he had bummed medication from jBoozy, he had taken some but become more tense with one, which was producing a tensinous problem requiring him to adhere to crazy mixed up martial arts relief, he tucked his left arm under himself as he was in his repose and got into reading all the info of the medications on the bottles he was taking, which was in such small print it required using a magnifying glass.

The exhaustive rhetorician he was, who at the call of answering the door, where was a tall man, Boozy had something to say.

He, later, hailed a couple who were having coffee at a donut shop while waiting for his order. They left it to him to answer. At the doctor's office group counseling, later, he talked.

"I was with them." said Boozy, "And as I was having coffee, I invited them to have coffee with me. That's all. I couldn't finish this large mug of coffee I had. At the bottom of the mug was a memory of having taken more medication than was specified. The coffee would be better after the take, but actually replaced it."

The doctor said, "Okay."

Then days later came along. At a picnic area the group of ex stoners hanging around before looking for a job talk was going on.

The subject of discussion by Zoong, Zong and Bo Nozy had gone to fight, which was off the subject, because it was while Leo and Boozy were entertaining something else.

Since an arm wrestling experience, which was seemingly non offending, non engaging was not a true, total fight, fight being an power emotion like thing could be sideput. The arm wrestling proceeded.

Although conflict in deciding which of two tables to use to do the arm wrestling proceeded, it was glossed over it didn't matter Then there was a decision on which of two empty tables at the outside picnic area to use. The table element was a choice made heavy, probably in connection to Leo's preference and Boozy's arm wrestling experience.

After the several arm wrestling sessions, one went to a number of draws which brought very loud cheers from their friends, Miss Minnie and Dr. Portini, the consideration of anything else was dissolving in the air and these two friends enjoyed a refreshing juice.

This was not a fight, nor would it in any way lead to a fight. It was a means to exercise. Both Leo and Boozy had arm wrestled before, Leo had indian wrestled, standing up in the hand hold, foot to foot, push pull contest, off balance loses, way. Off footing loses.

And if one loses, since they were unable then to immediately be standing up to catch baseballs and footballs, which was not good, it was but possibly neither a problem. One who wins is surely having no problem.

Two pair of boxing gloves landed on the table. Leo and Boozy both glanced quickly at the gloves. Mimi had returned from her car with them and tossed them to the side at the other end where the two had just finished.

Mimi said, "I got these at a thrift store but they're new. What do you think guys?"

Leo looked at them and replied, "They're oversized. There are no boxing gloves with that much padding anywhere. Where did you get them?

Mimi answered, "At the thrift store where I bought these."

She tossed a couple bunches of fake knives onto the table by the gloves. Once used as movie props, the knives blades, which were dull lightweight plastic, receded into the handles when pressed. Two of the other knives were both similar and appeared to be knife blades, but when pressed against any solid object bent, they were solid rubber, a soft rubber. They were supposed to be used in training self defense against an armed with knife attack and had gotten into the movie props that had been for sale.

Leo said, "Let's try on the gloves."

Boozy said, "Okay."

They proceeded to stick their hands in the oversized, overpaded gloves. Leo had his on first and lightly punched the picnic table, feeling how nice it was to have padding made him feel good. Boozy too tried to lightly press and punch the side of the picnic table. Soon Boozy and Leo were squared off, and the gloves were not tied. Boozy simply pressed the padding on Leo's arms and midsection. Then Leo punched Boozy in the noxe. Despite the thick padding, it caused Boozy to have a slight nosebleed. Mimi came to their aid somewhat as a referee would in a boxing match and talked to them.

Mimi, "I just wanted to show you guys this good buy. Give me the bloves. Oh, I hope you didn't stain it with your nosebleed."

Boozy replied, "It's okay. It stopped."

Boozy and Leo sat back down and looked at Mimi's stuff and at each other.

So the thought, 'fight for what' was in play. As two bystanders, Scott with his friend Travis who appeared to beg for a response, came around Boozy commented.

He said, "You wanna try?"

Travis said, "Anything for a little fun. No!"

Scott said, "Come on, let's give it a try?"

Travis replied, "Okay."

Now Travis and Scott looked at Mimi and she pushed the way oversized gloves toward them. Travis taunted Scott but not too seriously. They picked the gloves up, tried them on, leaving them untied.

Mimi commented, "If that Dr. Portini was around, he would like this."

Travis and Scott ignored her comment and squared off in the same area to the side of the picnic table where Boozy and Leo were sitting. Travis was a real tough guy, he had worked out a lot and no telling if he knew anything more about this thing, Scott was certainly no pushover but was forgetful, soft and probably wouldn't try this thing again ever.

First Travis patted his gloves together then threw a few light punches to Scott's shoulder area, which he blocked with his forearms. Then Scott came on strong trying to kill his friend. He swung his arms a little and landed a couple of punches. Travis, nonetheless replied with a few light punches, dancing around to make Scott work more. Scott threw a couple more kill punches (he gave an all, and to him it was a kill motivation) and started getting tired. Travis continued to land light punches on his friend. And they gave up conceding they were both tired.

With the gloves back on the table, and the group just relaxing after these events, Mimi picked these gloves and fake knives and put them back in her car.

The idea fight or flight, a theory in which a fight that seemed to happen could be avoided if wanted, was mostly in psychological formulations. It existed and was best taken existentially. Then it is best without expletives or the fight isn't likely in a theory of fight or flight, where anyone in the area of the fight is able to leave without a lot of expletives, which could be less.

There were times to consider, so Travis, who had wanted to engage Scott for the sport of it taunted him no more.

Travis taunted, "Touch my eyebrow hairs."

Scott took a wide arching right swing in his direction from about a yard away.

Travis felt a little wind pass by him from the swing and his moving his head and body back a few inches without moving his feet. Then, there was his joy, he was so far off, so far away.

If he could get Scott worked up emotionally, he might engage him with some stand up indian wrestling.

He looked around himself and said, "She continued to hold my hand."

Scott, Travis and Minnie were friends, Mimi being a girl and quite attractive had taken up with Travis in the past and Travis was boisterous about it.

The others, who had gathered and looked at the arm wrestlers, and there was a great pause bordering on mutual embarrassment for it, were quiet and respectful.

Scott continued, "She held it in her hand, on his lap, his hand and she pressed a little."

They were close but not that close. In fact Travis had a mental fantasy that accompanied his recurring mental psychoses. His delusions were undoubtedly to him real events happening or happened as the case might be he memorized them.

Travis went on, "I put my other hand, which was free and needed calming from its jittery, automaticity condition, to her forearm and lightly rubbed, it was pleasing her and actually relaxing me. She grabbed my rubbing hand quickly and I quickly pulled it back to my side quickly giving her the warmest smile I ever had given, which was the sweetest smile I could muster."

She was a smashing beauty! Right there!

"And I liked her." he went on. "She has a nice way of ducking to communicate. Real cute. And she was throwing out to me a feeling like of, like wow, this feeling I got is caught on you, to whom was affection."

"Well you should stay friends with her."

It's at night.

"And I wonder if she knows we are doing this. We could be squeezing each other's hands for ten minutes. The one love I knew of was excessively holding my hand."

The next week at Dr. Portini's office, there was a comment time. The others of the group therapy silently thought in an after meditation's ensuing quiet, somebody is helping us. The doctor, who controlled the lot, appeared and had his hat off. He snapped his finger. He paused. Everyone was back to normal.

And then Dr. Portini said, "Is there no hope for excessive hand squeezing?"

Boozy commented, "Is it like bed wetting?"

Minnie asked too, "Is it?"

Boozy ignored the question and said his piece, "If I had let you go on, it had got to stop, I said, let go, I would have said something else."

Dr. Portini commented, "Okay."

Boozy thought and loved it, commenting "And she had her way."

"And you held hands?" Minnie suggested.

The doctor became thoughtful and sought to release this client group at this group therapy. He was sitting on the option, thinking from his puzzlement. That puzzlement had seemed to come on him suddenly and he thought everything was okay.

The doctor said, "And if there is a way to help, you'll be okay."

Mimi, ballistically commented. That got to him. Mimi was fanning herself and talking. The mentality of the doctor, Doctor Portini, had back pages, mentally to himself. Mimi commenting, would come under the heading of too ballistic a comment, in the area of psychotic subconscious motivations. Consciousness of collective motivation included the psychotic unconscious and subconscious response. Psychotic thought showed on one of the faces in the semi circle.

The truth was in what Boozy asked. It was simple, can there be considered a thought that may be considered a memory of a ballistic comment in a consciousness blackout?

Mimi asked, "Got memory blackouts?"

Minnie said, "Psychotically thinking, at any particular point in time of a blackout, any point of time can constrain the effects of one to arrive at a consciousness, therefore these time points are non consciousness. See, the blackout has a map."

Some of the events in the group therapy went in the direction of the teaching a method of martial arts competition, and competitor mercy, this one loses it if it's in one's long distance blackout, was not out of the question of who it would be. The martial arts party reckoned it is a little like he envisioned, one who is infallible to a t was good.

Some of the group therapy attending members had been into a martial art discipline of Kate Juo, a mean style of martial arts where the teacher tells them these things they are supposed to do. The student was learning, like all the people in the semi circle, overhearing.

Leo said, with a mean, sarcstic smile, "Then it's all added up to points in a blackout to decide who wins?"

The doctor said, "I walked here. When I walked by some of the nearby houses a little boy came out of one and picked some object out of a mud puddle, he tossed it. He was playing. I thought, I hope that kid's mother is around. I glanced at the kitchen and rear room windows. They were curtained, but a mother's face peered out of one. I was glad she had an eye on the kid. Then, their dog barked. That's usual as dogs pick up scents and other things especially the way a person walks. I walk to avoid such clamor. Anyway, as dogs bark when they hear other dogs bark, other dogs barked too. The barking continued as I walked past the house. It trailed off as dogs barks do."

The doctor looked at Mimi and there was an icy silence for a short while. Mimi, who replied, was confident and good looking.

Mimi said, "Sometimes the kid comes over and knocks on the door. I ignore it in the middle of the day."

Dr. Portini lectured, "The eight hour workday allows it. The automatic thought release, which may be too much of a function for the psychopathic mind of a maniacal phobic martial art misguided practitioner is better left alone. I like it as it is, a psychologically understood cooking up to where the cooking is practice. That goes over to where the psycho or pseudo psycho can look back to their early motivation, give up and go home. That points us into the experience of challenge and asks, 'hey, is it okay?'"

Mimi could've gone into ballistic comments at this start of Dr. Portini stuff but she didn't. She was going self mind, inner, to trance-out on the opponent.

These small group therapy sessions continued for weeks. In these weeks, the house rocked by neighborly disco style parts regularly. The neighbor had stayed up all night and was habitually partying. Mimi's circadian rhythms got mixed up and they carried on in the normal daytime. Day after day. Mimi was become psychopathic as they were all but that bad. Their behavior toward all would be too bad and Mimi knew it. But since she could go into the sub behavior world and go on rather, call toward Leo, who was a tense person in a moment like that, and everyone had appreciated the pause, things worked out. The group therapy sessions maintained peace within. The meditation part of exercise was in group therapy transpired. This had been Dr. Portini's idea and it didn't turn out so bad. Boozy's inner look was eye strain for him but that was momentary.

As it turned out, the little boy had to quit playing when trucks drove past and he came to the house during off hours and said so.

"I won't play when the loud trucks go."

Leo was currently attending some of these sessions and reported.

Leo said, "More sexy, saner and safer."

Everyone looked at him and he retorted.

He said, "Look, I have a lot of headaches. I could see a doctor and my headache is gone. Finished."

Leo was of a successful completion of such a fine course of martial arts that if he breathed on someone, the excess of the martial arts school would help keep them away and to themselves. This was going to his foibles, which also helped him out.

Dr. Portini put it this way, "And do you approach him?"

In a martial arts arena he was sort of, just short of a match. It was theater provoking but he optimized out of the picture as the group therapist took over. So the session panned out toward its end when everyone would go home, as another great session rolled on to its end.

Boozy said something directly to his friends, Bo Nozy and Mimi, who came to his aid in friendship.

He said, "For me, perhaps looking at it as if we were on the set of a major motion picture, would help."

The session's events ensued with slight orientation, references to releases of indemnity were made but nobody paid much attention to it.

If palms were used, then, this month of a mention of martial arts at the session went on, it goes to the Jyne Tic school, which has a martial arts school of the Kuf Tuf school. Jyne Tic was constituent to Kuf Tuf! What might bring these groups to coming down was of hope to those who hoped to be seen.

In the signing and use of the release of indemnity, security for the event insurance in that is to allow the event. This level of even 'twas just what was recommended by seventy-nine percent of martial arts teachers interviewed, passed for near happening.

This forward momentum of reminiscences were on a dare by a martial arts school that has surfaced and asked for this party. They would jet down from their town and come into the place discussing the group effect of screening the aligned parties, which were as good, if set up with proper props, The unknowns watched as the promoters prepared a little alley section so no one would be hurt.

The martial arts catalogues and guide books were a wide vista of how not to be because these were the ways one didn't want to go, and were carried away by the many interested spectators, including some listening up dudes. Some were heavy!

Boozy said, "And this sent the thing into being done."

"But then," said Mimi, "I wake up to my own little scene, it's the delusion in the dream is the dream in the delusion. It's the scene."

Boozy commented, "I have this long range martial arts association to go to the past because it was like the martial arts school Kut Tuf. They said it was a link to psyched consciousness default and begged me to admit it is a proper thing to do to avoid craziness gain balance, confidence and if you win, money."

Dr. Portini added, "Events are the cornerstone of spacetime understanding." Leo said, "You're nuts."

Dr. Portini replied, "I'm looking for the nuts."

Leo said, "Some weird parties really wrecked me. Then some nearly did."

It was the third year of the events annual tricycle (over three years the events shift seasonally based on the four seasons to begin a new tricycle at the same place every three years.) and the mixed up martial artists contested he was a part of it. And Minnie was one of the most out to know people there were around there, she knew the schedule of events. She was there for the long faltering and needful huge bonuses at the end of the contests.

The psychology sessions helped. Somewhere, they were telling him that there was a tour for a year they could get into. If it was in the tri cycle of mixed martial arts, that allowed them to help others out of their quandary with the end of it being transportation was at the end of the line, most participants who had signed were into it.

Leo, who was good at winning martial arts contests, agreed it was a contemplation to strike that succeeded and was quiet.

Mimi mediated. Mimi advanced the proposition.

She said, "There a lot could be said about that."

Minnie said, "You guys should take look the martial arts stores. Be average, go there and buy the average of what they got. While there is a way out be into it. Do not let your attention go to the past or future. Be in the present."

This was a big thing for Boozy and Minnie. Leo was into it too. It produced an impression on Leo that was more than a real fact. It had an antipsychotic affect ringing in the atmosphere, all around it that made them all focus and think. Boozy thought focused.

Despite all the hash that it was developing to, Leo had to bite down hard for a seat at the talk in the group therapy. He was there.

Leo said, "Take it from me, at the end of the week, and we will all be together, it's ok."

They had seemingly angered of being sour, when they were taken to the place to watch and try and understand the implications of the do it again strategy they were purported to be witnessing.

Some of Leo's friends had it that if they walked out with the trophy all would be well.

Some of Boozy's friends said it was a very sudden piece of dialogue, but nevermind.

Boozy said, "Or it'll be good as a television program.'

This was not much to say with all the clamor. This was all he said and it was all Leo heard. Leo went ballistic. There was a pause as his headache departed, so they could all enjoy the group therapy for a while longer.

Five

It was early afternoon, eight before two. They were reminiscing.

Mimi said, "The next day after I took of the that was marketed for light weights, I had put on a few pounds and figured a would be my max. And besides these were very small compared to what another company marketed. It was the day before I had to go to the place where I might work, I lay in the backseat of my parked car and woke up. I sat up. Across the street in the yard were a few houses. The house right across had a driveway came plumb opened up toward where my car was parked. I was glad I had a room I could go to and really rest up in. They said, 'Dear, you'll have to come back tomorrow morning and we'll put you to work.'

Mimi and Minnie sat on a sofa with a guy in-between them. And he put an arm around each. Leo was happy.

It wasn't long, but before they all had left, and found their work, they looked back. Boozy helped out in a garage where painting was part of the services offered. Safety was first and safety inspectors inspected the place occasionally.

But he was happy on his own and would find his best times at his own home.

"Then, I thought, good, my room was close to the landlord, who was gone away for a week to visit friends and relatives across the state and I could get up early, drive there, rest over in my car. You would like to work?" So Mimi was parked there for the better part of a day. She, watching the light change as the sun came up. It had been cool, it was cool and there was a breeze.

Boozy stopped by seeing her car and commented out the window to her open windows.

Boozy loudly said, "I was hoping we could go somewhere to do some shopping or eat. But I didn't know if you'd be up to it so I went searching in the yellow pages for a new coffee maker. Perhaps I'd have to get the feeling I had before to make some coffee? Here I am."

Mimi answered, "I was going to go through with hanging out here longer but I didn't. I was a bit stunned by finding someone else being here all night. At least I had been coming to the communing with nature." "Lot of trees around." Boozy answered.

"And I found conversation in the sun rays coming through the clouds and the wind breezing in the day through the trees. I felt life and I felt goodness. I was eavesdropping on nature"

It was early when Dr. Portini was getting up and heading toward his office, which was next door to where a client of his was resting in their car. That client gonna work me, he thought It was going to be another typical day with an early arrival at a busy office. Busy for this psychologist was no one had arrived yet, except the receptionist and first client.

Boozy was a stout first in for a consult.

And he said, "Little did I fully realize it like I liked to consider, but I was thinking very heavy, some were supposed to have, I mean i almost took of at once, so what am I worried about?"

She said, "We s a long time ago."

"Ya. Who'd you with?" asked Boozy.

"That was racking up a good round of applause." said the doctor. He opened the door. The receptionist-assistant was right there.

The assistant continued, "As an ex stoner, you should know that your best experience portfolio is the least of possibilities. So when the portfolio is for something else, it is the way. When you're looking at it as the way it is and it altered your view, wait.

There was a knock on the door.

Boozy commented, "I knew one hip cat."

With more, all bummers, when they were just tightening their belts with regard to concern for this or that experience. There was this one cat. He was quite onto having these numerous experiences with this or that friend. Experiences that were supposed to be special, were additives to an right-on time with a from south of the border theme.

Some things were ocean.

Dr. Portini said, "There was one cat wanted us to believe there were a few rare, certain fish that contained psychedelic potential. Ya."

Boozy looked at him, smiled and said, "I'm sticking with what I got, doc. And none of it is your business nor on that list of things you call things that get one high and heaven bound. I never heard of no such fish."

The session was soon over and Dr. Portini invited Boozy to dine with him nearby in the office building's snack shop.

They were there when Minnie came into the small lunchroom, which was reserved for office holders and their patrons, and the assistant doctor and her ex stoner clients.

Those who wanted some help in getting guidance got past the denial and got it, and getting guidance, and wanting guidance was through their time of post using, which was actually going to take up the rest of their lives.

Minnie said, "One person I liked was his client from the suburb, it was Mimi."

Mimi answered, "She was never before in her life like that, or most. We had not once been experimenting with with some strange and, and had a few friends similarly experienced."

She felt guilty and though she had a strong denial. It was so strong that she herself had guilt feelings that could bother her. So she took an appointment with Dr. Rodgers. He was a specialist in the guilt and denial area. He had had a sense of these things. He had worked out of a rehab and had a private practice.

Mimi had a part time job in a retail shoe store.

Someone relaxed in the waiting room outside the doctor's office, a lobby in a large building. This, it was not inclined as a time deluded me for years, he thought.

"Would it ever be the year two thousand?" asked Dr. Rodgers.

And if it got too icy. The bony, stoney would have no idea where all the rest of the gang, some with years off even in psychedelic tales, were."

"Or if they were still tripping with bong. Are you alright?" Dr. Portini cordially asied.

Nor did he know if any of the majority of them who used some of the things he had used. He came along his ways of success nonetheless.

That Mimi tried to remember my bummers was a personal assessment of things because they all liked to write diaries like they were personal pronouncements to the people in them.

"Some of them were stuck into a doctor's office and came out the other side, okay."

He sat down and buried his head in his hands, shutting out the world despite embarrassment and possibly being labeled and ostrich, and changed his mind on looking up, from looking at the majority of magazines, several he had open to similar ad pages or articles that fit in well, and read for a moment. Good things and God were there. He was in luck. He was there to see the doctor.

"The next day, toward the end of the day they were extremely well suntanned, to say the least, and they couldn't see working. Mimi saw a familiar face across the street and for several weeks came there to at least remember having seen her friend. They saw a lot of greenery, the sky was grey, the trees were tall and nature was tough. It looked as though it was about all through with having the many experiences she'd had.

"I'd never hallucinated until I took a look at nature." She said to Dr. Rodgers. "It allowed me to see much more of what I didn't know was there, which was something to be real aware about. I was seeing nature everywhere I looked. It was real nice. I saw a rainbow. Nature was there and I wondered why I didn't go somewhere to work."

The doctor agreed to recommend work therapy.

Her friend Boozy came in with their own experience. He sat in the waiting room just like others.

Inside, he reported to the doctor, "That experience of mine one year was that bad. It was in a parking brake on experience and my car was used. That was while there were years of that were in the wind and I saw that were going to turn me into a sponge. I was through with non real. I went to growing up."

Doctor Rodgers politely nodded. Boozy nodded back.

Doctor Rodger's said, "You're almost ruminating, my friend."

So Boozy went on, "I didn't take too much. I knew a girl took some. I was taking one after another, she had said. Then the question came up to me in some years later, which I came to agree was too much drug use. It was really possible those were years to really be holding on to."

"I didn't use to take it any more than I had to. I did it to cure myself of anything else iI didn't see. It was really possible, something else was never going to happen again, so I was into it. I wasn't about to understand how it might have been taken by some low status people. It got to me most of the people who were asking for it were the drug inventors. They discovered recently it was something good, so they, possibly thought it was best in the class. And I sure wasn't about to get into history books. They say the alchemy is real good with some of that stuff and ancient goals have been reached."

There were street sounds, the screech of cars where the driver suddenly pressed the gas pedal mostly.

"It was beginning to let up when they got heavy again." said Boozy.

Three came in the door. Boozy to Benny or Bully or Buddy or Buddy or Bud- another party, the leisure between parties was the heading we were on.

Hailing a panhandler was something only a guy like Zoong would do.

There was a person, Zoong, who had said something to his friend Mimi. She was giving a party.

She said, "I am having a party next thursday night and I'd like you to come. You're welcome."

"Thank you." he replied.

He thought she had said 'hi' to the man who was walking by them when he, the man, had saluted him with a friendly, disarming salute. That would have been nice. A woman standing up for a man has a lot to say for it.

The man said something as a guy like Zoong, Zong walked on in. Boozy, the man, having recognized Zong from one of Mimi's house parties, commented positively.

He said. "Hi, you all. Nice day, isn't it?"

Zong was offended. But Boozy, being bigger and stronger, did not even notice. If it hadn't been for Mimi's comment, Boozy would have not even paused. Zong, too, appeared to let it pass. He let his offensive attitude reduce to enjoyment of the party.

Mimi asked him, "What are you doing this fine day?"

"One of the most memorable events I have ever had is," said Boozy, "is when it's having someone interesting being cool and interested in you."

Zong didn't blink, but he was listening.

He asked, "You being interested in me?"

The next day party was at Mimi's house.

This was soon inside at Mimi's party and he was getting comfortable. Boozy, too was leaning back in his chair. Zong couldn't find anything to say and nodded to Boozy occasionally. Boozy thought, that means something. Zong was interested in a handout, but was too proud to exactly say he needed a few dollars to make ends meet that day.

"Okay." said Boozy.

This was Boozy's way of staying the event without getting into anything with anybody except Mimi, whom he was attracted to. Mimi liked him, but more as a friend than a lover.

Mimi was there along with friends. A friend was cleaning the place up and getting a little ready for the soon influx of her friends to the party.

They came and listened to records. Boozy was outspoken. He said some things to Zong. Zong nodded. They listened to Boozy for quite a good while as he went on. He wasn't too loud or abrasive, neither sharp nor too understandable or incoherent.

"I got the feeling every time I inhale something other than what I enjoy, I'm going to regret it." Zong said.

Mimi replied, "Me too. Keep breathing like you do."

It wasn't exactly a party, the party had been the week before.

Spare change was not a source of money, it was a means to self esteem. Having a spare change moment did something. Mimi managed as did Boozy Thaz, the regular friend to ask someone who they had ever before been out with. He met, for a financial hand out of an undisclosed sum in which a minimum of coin would be realized, i.e. one cent, Zoong.

Soon this someone else was there, Zoong. He strangely had no thought of initiating a long term coin take, much less a financial sum in which he could realize there was a way to get by without going through a temporary work office.

Zong asied Mimi, "This Boozy, was he a gentleman? Is he a large person?"

Boozy was there. Mimi was then aware of Boozy. She offered him more drink, which was more than Boozy, who was actually entertained by being just over a hangover in which he didn't know what it was he was hungover from, had had recently. She also offered him a side dish, potato chips.

Boozy thanked her and dug in.

"Thank you, Mimi. I needed that."

Nonetheless, Leo, who knew him as Mr. Thaz referred to him as Boozy. Leo knew him when he was sober, which was nearly all the time since he had been to counseling for substance abuse.

Out by the street some strangers were hailing party comers, most of the party comers gave some spare change. The strangers thanked them as their tally increased.

Some panhandlers took their time! There is a moment of minimum initiation in which the panhandler seeks a space off of financial realization, a peace of a mind space, where in their obtaining some spare change is a momentary space, a part of spacetime, without the time, they are elated. Attention! Responding positively is peace. Positive was the hand out. The person who gave them some change was interested in becoming so elated and did, in fact, experience an elation in handing out their pocket change, which was actually lightening the load in their pockets. Some of them handed over whole handfuls of small denominations of coins. Everyone was happy.

"Hey, Boozy." Zoong said, softness in his voice increasing as he said the name so there was hardly an audible ending to his hailing Boozy by name.

Since some time was gone by since Boozy or Zoong had interacted, by Boozy's appearing and decisive comment which was inspiring to Zoong, they were both forgetting it, that they had an acquaintanceship. Time was in a normal importance area to them.

Time goes by them, Boozy looking at a person as someone to panhandle. Then, when panhandling is transpiring, eye to eye contact is made. Boozy has his, the moment of panhandle time transpires to having the panhandling down pat. A panhandler knows panhandling and that allows the panhandling to be an experience of antipsychotic action, a psychological schizophrenia breaker. For one to have relief from such an onset in which paranoia causes a twofold psychosis, giving to the panhandler is one of the best things they can do for their mental health,

Boozy is one of the people the panhandlers, who minding their own business, relates to. One becomes a soft panhandler to do good. Others may need bus fare somewhere. And two dollars, being fairly often panhandled, is often requested by the panhandler. It was a relief to the schizoid who got panhandled.

The psychosis steps into the direction of paranoia by both the panhandler and the panhandled. Spare change is a way out.

Boozy thought this Boozy. Thatch thought he should establish a high amount of some sort of personal presence. And change resource.

Boozy Thaz was similar to this Mr. Thatch. Bozzy. was a halting figure, in Boozy's experience halting the ongoing tide of paranoid schizophrenia was interesting.

He enjoyed counting his change, separating it to denominations for use. He planned to save. He knew Mimi Casey and respected her for that. She managed her spare change better than he did. But she would not buy his cockamamey false money scheme, which was a bottle cap collection. He had hundreds pounded out on an anvil, filed safe and bagged. Someday there'd be a market and he'd sell out. He thought.

Some ex-stoners gathered embracing rehabilitation, hanging out in regular places. Mimi was one of the ex stoners.

Also there was Boozy Thaz. Of the ex-stoners, who told a story of their being hailed, Mimi Casey talked of some guy who owed her because he had said he'd loan her about a hundred dollars.

Mimi had gone to a party where a group of stoners and ex-stoners hang out. Some ex stoners talked among themselves, some ex stoners also were straggling in from curbside automobiles, hanging out in the two car garage that opened to the house living room.

One man pawed the pillow next to where Mimi was sitting. She looked at it. He said something to her.

The man said, "How are you?"

Once before, when she was smashed at a party, she met a similarly looking man, who became a long time friend.

Again, she had come to the house when there was a soft party, a few people. She had come from the busy party where she had been hailed by the man who looked like her long lost friend. She was of a party at the party.

Mimi was hailed again.

The dude said, "Hey."

She was sitting on a sofa and someone across the floor glared at her, waved to her, came to her and asked her her name.

She said, "Mimi."

Some ex stoners hanging out outside the garage had gathered for a while enjoying after mealtime company. The most part of them were satisfied to spend about half an hour there and leave.

Mimi walked around, she walked out to the street and back.

Passing the stragglers, she goes on to find out that there is someone who is hailing her, who had previously followed her to her car. He hid behind another car and daringly peeked so she'd see him. She wasn't running from him.

And if one is showing off that one is hailed, they walk further. She had a walk from her car to further away from the party before abruptly changing her course of away to her car. To her car was close. Away from the strangers.

They at the party were some once smashed group and being themselves.

The difference between the person who hailed and the group of the party, who were startled, was in a calm excitement bordering sexual excitement, which is where being hailed resulted in responding by making, slightly, subtle, warm faces. With trusting, everything is alright, will be alright, as demand for non attention is with caution.

She is assumed by the one hailing, to be read up on all the news. She stands by the one who hailed. The one who hailed seems lost.

One such as Mimi looks at a party before leaving, and high tailing it home as is her manne, rather than a reporting response to being hailed by a stranger, who is influenced by the party atmosphere, sat comfortable at the party she returned to in mind, actually it was a bus stop. The hailing was repeated by then. She had felt good at the party and so was comfortable at the bus stop.

The ex stoners from a rehab group therapy were at the party and spent some time going into spare change consciousness, spare changing anyone to get a few dollars together. It occurs regularly for those seeking self esteem that way. One who pays may find out they are going to experiencing life beyond before giving because they're without some money they had. But they were reconnecting successfully.

Then somebody was hailed.

Being hailed was a check on his inclusion in the party.

A Doctor Drewe Portini hailed Boozy Thaz. He saw him before leaving the party. They were both leaving. It was with a fast exchange of glances.

A knowing glare preceded a friendly word. "Hey" said Dr. Drew Portini, a man known as Mr. X for all Boozy knew.

Boozy kept walking but slower. "What?" He asked.

Drew Portini, the hailer, let it go.

"For a while we were keeping in touch by mail." the strange Drew rather seriously said.

Boozy replied, "What mail?"

Then the doctor continued talking, like one out of some great rumination to be appreciated.

Dr. Portini said, "And I made up a number. Then I got your telephone call! When will I see you?"

"Whenever." replied Bozzy softly, "This is the number, _____.

He said it so softly, he wasn't sure it was audible. This was all he had to do. It sounded like he had made up the phone number to Dr. Portini

Bozzy reiterated, "My number is there when you want it."

Dr. Portini produced a very small pad and pen to write the number down.

Bozzy produced a number, "1,000,000,000" he said softly.

Drew scribled the number and put the tiny pad and pen in his trouser pocket.

Following the small party, then, one person named Bob talked to another person, Bob.

"Bob." said the other Bob.

A conversation proceeded with nobody knowing anything more than they had before the conversation. Bob and Bob went their ways. A few days later Bob was having a lunch with his friend Bob at the restaurant place.

Bob asked, "Did you talk to that Zoong?"

Bob replied, "He came out of nowhere to stay overnight in the living room."

Bob said, "Tell me about it."

Zoong, Bob's friend, might be next to have to report on. Mimi went to her friends with that some kind of a person was hailing her story. Zoong, who she had briefly met at one of her parties, then met up with her at a street corner after another small party at friend Ethel's house and after being at a friend's house. She went to Ethel's house.

"He telephoned my number, hung up, and then I waited." said Ethel.

The others listened and smiled at Ethel. Mimi coaxed a description.

"Come on, Ethel, did you meet this man?"

"Yes. He was with me, he was going to stay for awhile." Ethel said.

The others who had watched him leave early from the party sat a little more comfortable then. Zoong had come and gone and come again.

When he came again to the party it was the next day, he knew he'd be okay. He sat down and cracked a few pecans on the porch and ate them. Then, he smiled purposefully and took three almonds out of his fanny pack, set them down and one at a time cracked them open with one whack each, not without expending a quote to the inhabitants at the party inside.

Inside the house, the screen door was closed and latched, Mimi and her friend Ethel were talking.

Pretty soon there was a crack, the sound of an almond breaking from the force of Young's slapping it against the porch step siding, a smooth concrete area where he sat with the almond between his spread legs. He hit the next almond as it lay flat with the side of his palm, turning his hand just before the impact so the muscle on the side of his palm would tense up and absorb the semi sharp anti pressure of the almond shell. Zong was able to eat a few almonds. He tried a pecan, and similarly enjoyed the pecan.

Zong had been eating peanuts in the shell again and was enjoying cracking a few nuts before he left.

Mimi came out. Fresh from the kitchen, she held a nine inch knife by its blade, sharp point away from her palm. She walked to the end of the concrete porch raising her hand with the knife, and flung it down at the pile of miscellaneous nut peelings beside the porch on the bare dirt earth. The turn of her hand as she let go of the blade was just enough to allow the sharp point of the knife to rotate one hundred and eighty degrees as it sailed down pretty quickly, with a good deal of force, into the miscellaneous nut shells Zong had swept aside over the previous weeks.

"Bye, Mimi." he said.

Inside the conversation continued. Zong walked slowly to the sidewalk, did a weak left face and continued walking very slowly. Mimi went back inside.

"What about the man, Ethel?" Mimi asked.

"Anyway, he's helping with the rent, and he'll beat stranger company." Ethel said.

She talked about the man she was letting sleep in her living room. Mimi was having a similar situation at her house.

Mimi replied, "We set up kitchen for a while when he came, me and the others where I live. Then he left for a few days. There were weekly meets after that and then he would come back he said."

Several times the stranger knew where he was welcomed at. Ethel was well aware that she had been headstrong in denying his welcome at times. The stranger came and went.

"They have had this rhetorical ramble all lined up. Perhaps he was conditioning me, perhaps he was hypnotizing me, perhaps he was just out of some mental ward and had been in mental conditioning?"

The next week, Ethel was walking home from Mimi's and enjoying her walk home. Someone was set to rendezvous with her at a bus stop. The stranger, who was becoming familiar to her, had a bright side.

"We're psychotic." the stranger said.

Then he sat down. And he indicated this with a psychotic nature he had. Once, by saying things are like, well, not that bad, and it would be hard to pin down if it was that bad.

"He hailed me from the midday shadows, the nearness to a business store wall outside was lurking someone as I walked." said Mimi. "It was him. He was like some cowboy guy I might have seen riding off into the sunset in a movie as it ended."

Boozy said, "Uh huh."

"Like many of my friends he was okay but just so-so. He became a token from the shadows of life, good for transportation but not to be overused, not too good to be expensive. But it was me, he was in my continual psychosis but he was that guy who saw he was just a stranger. No one was with me at the right time. But he was there. Often. And no one saw that he gave me a cold look, which was when I was gathering some strength to have faith that there were so such odd things as flying carpets, or characters in the world on the walk I was living who met up with his own things from an assortment of people."

"The stranger Boozy. came to see me and rest from travel.

"He wasn't all o.k." said Boozy.

Zoong went inside and sat. It wasn't a large place and Boozy commented to anyone around, but somewhat where Zoong was resting.

Boozy said, "Cough syrup was to control the fever that the mosquitoes gave him; also, it's giving me a means to assuage my headache that comes on me at the wrong time."

If Boozy had not been there, he would have said, uh huh. The small party at Ethel's was taking off. Mimi was talking to her friend Ethel at Ethel's house in her living room and Ethel told her about her encounter with the stranger.

Ethel said, "Ya, Mimi. You listening, Boozy? That guy was lurking in the shadows."

Mimi said, "I read labels, I follow instructions on labels. You don't drink cough syrup. That guy says he drinks cough syrup straight from the bottle. Not okay."

He drank some more cough syrup from his bottle. Just a sip and tightened the cap.

Mimi went on, "I watched.

"The next day I saw him leaving a restaurant and he stayed talking to this guy, could have been a delusion because I heard the guy was someone he wasn't likely.

"So I go out for a few days and next thing, it's him next to the building shadows.

"At home, later, I found my usual stack of bills come from easy living, which were to only be getting paid through piecemealing, which is what I got to do to be honest.

"The stranger would help"

Ethel enquired, "Would it become he was a nutcase?

Mimi answered with a question, "And would he become the landlord?"

He was hoping so.

Ethel continued to the third degree, "The landlord your friend, Mimi?"

The person who hailed Bozony was then at a party from where he would be going to his well being therapy. He also hailed Mimi.

Boozy called Ethel, who was on the other side of a picnic table where they were then having lunch. The stranger walked away.

"He was a little hyper or something." Mimi said to Bozony.

Inside their tent, which they had purchased together for day park shelter, was a boombox. It was off, loaded with fresh batteries and newly acquired interesting CDs. Bozony reported the event to Mimi.

"He hailed me the late morning, the sun was near noon so few shadows were around. He came of a business as I walked by on my way from shopping." said Boznoy. "He was like so many of my friends, so-so. He's became taken from the shadows of life. But he was just a with me at the right time. And that gave me a cold, which was gathering some strength.

"Cough syrup was to control gave him; also it's giving me a headache time. I stayed the building stack of bills only through piecemealing what I got."

Would it become a case? And would he become the therapist? He was hoping so.

Bonzy stood outside Mimi's tent door and hailed Bonzy five times over about half as many minutes. Still no answer.

A host of visitors appeared and started becoming involved with the couple and then some.

"It would be good to go and see them." said Mimi. She was not far from the tent entrance. On the inside. Boozy was there.

"Coming to visit him!" she said in self-amazement. "It's okay."

Zong had returned.

"Guess so." Zong replied. "And I'm glad it's us who are going to be talking to them there, but I've got to hail Bonozy. If it's him,. Those, who it's not so okay to be with, agree. But I like him. And that is okay with me, they're all pretty good people to be with..."

"And so, yet the next day comes."

Muze replied very confidentially, "If you were saving money by hailing someone, and I would believe it would be a good idea to do., you'd be okay."

"At three. He'll be there. He knows it. It's to unload the debt retrieval. He expects it at the continuing of our work week walk."

"And his is non-stop?"

Private Martial Artists | 69

"I tried to be nice. he said, the last time. But because he was incapable of hanging out, I said some nice things about food. It set him up, once, into a good mood."

"I was not out of the way."

"His use of poverty was but just first class rhetoric. It was paramount. And so interesting, even though it was difficult to handle at times."

Bozny was right there, "I tried to stay right on with the food line, but at times they just tried to stay the flow of the conversation we were having. It was an angry approach."

"It had been his lecture that interested me. And we had to talk to him to begin with. I had said, not anything about it is going to get through to him, though I may have been wrong. He phoned my mother and let her know I was here. And then there are still of small loans I sorta made to him. Nor would it be good, but I said, I will see you are making notes on what they was saying, so okay. Here's your five."

"I have been through a lot of that kind of stuff, hoping for things to get better. But with him it was too much to ask. But from his table, which was unbelievably well supplied with refreshments, an appointment for me to keep was the cold, which was something I was used to."

There was no escape since it was just me serving up my sense of judgement," Bozzy replied. "Which probably could have used more than just a good tongue-lashing. But who's confusion is it?"

"Perhaps you should have been going in a much too much relaxed direction? Zong asked.

"His presence there tensed me up more than I cared to be. It got to me all over."

"With him there wouldn't be a little conversation?"

"Better at meals."

An opportunity to go meet someone looms. Someone else remembers acquaintances and of course the company of the meeting. Some can go, I was like that, at least since we was here and not there. But it seems there was a little man in each of us.

"My life was a better with friend than not. So I've had to go it in a long run with time to spare. And I felt sorry for him since he could not shut up." Zong folded his hands and sat back across the table from Mimi, hiding his glaring.

"Where's my power?" asked Mimi.

"And where's my friend?" replied Bozzy.

"And it seems as long as he was calling me from somewhere!" _____ said.

Boozy replied, "Nowadays, it comes and goes."

They went to the job and got working at it, but as it was they were about through.

"And since then," Mimi replied, "I met with my friends who I told not to come to the lake..."

"They came back and left me. And I came back here until the last time I had called and asked him if they didn't want to come out. Not going, come back from rehab, yet had me sad. And I was all for refunding them five dollars for this cab ride out. But it got to me. And I was somewhat psychotic with mental reservation about guilt self-consciousness motivation."

"He had with him his good nature, though it was all but what I had." said Muze, who had conferred with the doctor before leaving for the day,

Doctor Portin had been her first connection.

She had retired from the outing to the lake to openly advance a pseudo practice about the wild outskirts through a coffee wagon. Though she was out, she kept a connection with the doctors, who actually disapproved of her going with a lack of civility.

And her main patient, who had a lack of ability to converse with anyone, Bonzy also said that he wasn't so okay.

Bonzy went on. And then got exasperated, "But who am I to talk."

"He could talk and I could listen," she reported to her doctor friends. "But I wanted to converse and there was no point in going on." she said about one of her clients. "He wouldn't listen."

"I am in three psychotic collective subconscious groups here. They told me you would not hear from me again unless I have the memories of what, for all that they are worth, pays." said Zong.

And his voice shears off part of the world they all knew as it seemed to be falling apart. Zong was reckoning of an evening was noteworthy. It upped the score and seemed to be a falling out, apart from any known event, or as far from a perfect order of God that offers real change that one could get.

"Through psyching up?" asked Bozny.

He was mentally falling apart and it seemed like he always was a little mentally out of synch, and he always will be. But it was a mental passing time. Something, generally, all who are released go through.

The telephone rang once on a weekend. It was him.

"And as if his mother had come over from the neighbors, I was mainly startled." said Bozny. "And so I reviewed my notes from his previous phone calls. Most of them were about him."

"And with his mother there, which gave him some added time to support our friendship, I and my six partners, who were giving him best wishes for the fun of it, suggested it was best for him." said E. Nego.

Bonozy replied, commented on with what Dr. Portini had once said,

"Too much! Dr. Portini had always said, 'you try to get through to someone so that you all are better.'" said Boozy.

They were in touch. If it wasn't happening, you really should let it go was the thought. If he is all to himself, and it's in any or all possible psychopathic directions, they're in the collective subconscious collectives in which they have set it up for themselves to be.

As one, himself, hails it is to be there. Someone hails and you can't get through to them. Best to let it out and let them know it's good to not be psychotic. In not all cases, this works. In my opinion this is best.

Bonozy suggested, "So as he went on seeing clients he succeeds in getting a lot of them to a condition where they're appearing normal and gainfully employed. Usually extensively!"

The doctor was aware.

She stopped there while the rest of them seemed to have gotten it all figured out.

"It was still seemly possible to me that she might have had to have a control on his identity crisis without really being his friend." said Uzz. "But I dropped the idea that weekend they decided to go back to the luck and didn't. I can voice good references. This, he, had been helping with the food, and that's what their bag of groceries was about."

Dr. Portini replied, "I was very unconcerned about the likeliness that food or that drink which was food, helped you."

replied, "it usually occupied most of my mind."

That we can hang out some and wine it was so cool bringing it on foot a chore because we moved out in the boonies. you're out of town I will say about work so bring out the food though they are working that have little tiny problems that go with it to me and he directly to town down but as it was other."

Mimi said, "And again I meet my friend. And that guy. I told him not to come back and he believed me. That's everything!"

It seemed to be okay and he had gone his way a better person. His paging was once, we're going on to my bedroom for my living room experience. Or perhaps you want it the other way around, and to find out I'm paging you."

Six

These heads were into milk therapy.

Hitchers had come, recklessly hailing for their rides and getting the needed transportation. And therapy.

Accidental death was about to happen. Those like the reckless driver type, in the assessment by Bonozy to Dr. Portini, could be false.

Boozy and Ethel had hitchhiked together to a sparsely populated small town. They sat at a bus stop by an empty lot on a block with a lot of empty lots, looking at the dry earth. It cracked as such mud does when it dries.

The tectonic plate treatment took place in a virtual reality campsite under the auspices of a group in a virtual reality life that was sponsored by Dr. Portini. From the very beginning, this recovery from a non happening clinic on the outskirts of the small town, which had a little more life, was a gas station event. And so there was a blame for the cracks on the earth that went to a tectonic plate deeper as a sign of the potential.

Those who were within love were with someone who had come to a room in this house for therapy. Some of the group were there. Soon Mimi said something.

She said, "He had heard of love therapy."

This was at the group, love therapy, small though its attendance was, Boozy, Mimi and Dr. Portini, there was a means to a continued procedure of their conversation. Dr. Portini swore it helped, raising his hands to high heaven.

He said, "This is great.".

Mimi commented, "Boozy and I once hitched around. He said his brothers, Bonanza and Bonozy were in a homosexual relationship, which was once touted to cure the oedipus complex, which they both had a touch of."

"That blew it, Mimi." said Dr. Portini.

There were a few moments of quiet as they all smiled.

"This is madness." said Boozy.

"That's the theater went the other way." Dr. Portini snapped.

"Well bless the frogs." Mimi said smartly.

Dr. Portini had to tell her where to get off. Those kinds of comments were incendiary to say the least a bit metaphorically.

Then, with other friends one or so times, we hitched, again and as one might expect it, we met others who hitched around."

Bonozy added, "Some of them were set up to go out and hitchhike and some were hitchhiking as a professed professional."

"That's right, Boozy." Buzzy went on. "On this hitch circuit, you would wake up and go out to hitchhike, usually meeting some professional people as talented as they were, going about their business, driving places."

"Hi." said Bonozy, "I am moving seats, so everyone will have a place to sit."

Mimmie replied, "In the few years before becoming that acquainted with the street hitchers and al it was heroic to do it, we found no one about. And in a few short weeks of the usual hitchhiking, it was a gone scene. Good, to meet someone some other time. Or else maybe Minnie and Mimi remembered?"

Minnie, sitting quietly was patient, "But what does all that mean? Someone asking if perhaps he looked nervous was up in the air. It was making me a little more nervous than I should be? But then, being like that was, in its way, what I was echoing in doing what we did."

"I walked around visiting areas for the arrival of these passenger hitchhikers." said Mimi.

Boozy, getting nervous, listened to jets in the distance.

He said, "As we were near an airport once we paused in a garden park and looked forward to being back home with friends. We were probably listening to the same records. When I was around a stereo, I felt like a goldfish in a large pond."

"Those are carp." Mimi said.

"For me," Boozy harped in. "It's camp."

Boozy started listening to birds chirping something about a new record for length of time it didn't happen. On the other than at the end of the road, which was a concept, the rest of the group connected with the gist of the group therapy purpose, in this case, with love in mind.

Mimi said, "Our company ended at a park. It was better than a few other places to be at."

Boozy supported Mimi's bent, "Others came and went."

"They had to visit us, they were probably very high." said the big hearted, Boozy Thaz.

The group therapy was going to be replaced by milk therapy if the doctor ever got it together. A Dr. Spontane had come up with it and he was visiting the group. He came.

Dr. Spontane said, "You can make a therapy out of just about anything. So I offered the executives where I work a proposal that I would come up with milk therapy. No one had heard of it before and I knew it would be good. You'd start with bathing your feet in a shallow pool of milk"

The clients were soon pouring in for the therapy they thought would help them.

Dr. Spontane said, "Some of them, who were later found quite alright and had taken some milk therapy, came back for another round of sessions. First they bathed their feet in milk for a half hour, that used milk would be washed down the sink, then they'd get a ten ounce glass of cool milk."

Dr. Spontane approved of this approach and said he'd like to see some of them drink the unpasteurized milk.

Dr. Spontane said, "We want unhomogenized, fresh, not pasteurized milk. It has to be fresh."

Dr. Portini, who was happily enjoying the benefits of a cool glass of fresh, unhomogenized, non pasturized milk, which was available from a specialty store he knew, responded with a proposal that, the client might like too. He'd decide by stepping in controlled puddles of unpasteurized unhomogenized milk that there was a positive benefit in doing that.

"Milk is life. And so we love the cow." He said.

Less than an inch of milk was about seven ounces in a narrow pan. The layer of unhomogenized milk for half to a whole hour, then, gave its nutrients and cleaned the feet. Soon, the milk would be disposed of down a sink. After soaking for a while, at least half an hour, the client could take a drink of milk.

There should be some other ways to use milk in therapy thought Dr. Spontane.

"I'll sleep on it." he said.

Dr. Spontane replied, "Okay."

Some of the clients there had hitchhiked a little ways on a busy street to get there. One of them was stopped by a police patrol car.

The two officers parked their car and got out and walked to the sniveling hitchhiker and started asking routine questions. The hitchhiker was being questioned for a murdered, by a reckless driver, hitchhiker. Buzzy, who was there had hitchhiked.

That would get to me." said Buzzy. "It, got to me."

The first officer told him this was possibly an accidental hitchhiker, possibly by his own carelessness in standing close to rush hour traffic fault.

The other officer said, "In me was a feeling. We would not want to be the guy."

"If he was from my high school, whose girlfriend had called and gotten a grand from my savings account for a release of their possessions from a safe deposit box when they had lost their key. My parents, he said, were thoughtful and loved being of the group.

"Somebody hailed him?"

The group therapy session that had started without Buzzy. But it was soon happy to see him walk in as normal.

Marnie commented, "There were other times, which had recently been had. When we was having a housewarming, his parents came to give us a lot of records from their past." she started getting giddy. "And all my stoned wallflower type friends are there."

"Bonanza said it was going to be an all night party." said Buzzy.

"I will be all situated there once the apartment gets set up. Okay?" asked Bonozy. "Sometimes, it is moot."

They looked around, Mimi asked, "Are you in?"

Bonzy replied, "We'll just keep the other apartment because at this particular party, everyone is going home early. Some girls, I guess, will be keeping it interesting for a while."

The doctors and their therapies were out of the picture when the group gathered spontaneously for a get together. Mimi was early to arrive and had some milk to drink.

Boozy came in, he said he had just had milk.

The fun loving party went deep in the main part of the psychotic subconscious collectives. One could guess that a party was on someone's mind but it wasn't that much of a psychosis collective subconscious of a party with a whole lot goers then.

Some more people experiencing it were thinking this is too stony for even a stoner.

The communication of a mental telepathy type was from an area. With it was a stillness. The party, with the few hip people; went and left. All them people of the small party were gone. Some of them went to the bathroom? One or two stuck around but weren't there. So it was all too much. It was a stroke of luck someone left the records biy the record player. Someone stuck to it there.

"If that was that it was apparently about all?" Mimi asked.

"It will be dozens of years before you would think about them parties again, Zong." said Boozy.

Thought, about the dangerous hailer, the, a, stranger came up. It was in response to the mention of a murdered by an apparent hit and run reckless driver hitchhiker and someone was questioned.

"About how long will it be? We're out and we lie about a biography. It's an autobiography even though it will be spied upon."

Friendship was also to be found in a friendship ring, where most all the friends were well and into being in the collective subconscious of friendship, where they were automatically liked. Friendship was also from the likeness, as of the properties in which a reptilian attitude toward life and friends existed coming and going. These were living friendship beings who were conscientious as some, always conscientious. They all, also, came to have their share.

They all had their eyes on an empty gazebo nearby, somewhat a reminder of a rehab they had been to recently as a guest of Dr. Portini for a day. And a part of the coffee truck's territory! A fence about the pavilion was facing the others, who were recently released, it was ornamental parly about the pavilion. Minnie had accompanied them.

Minnie found it interesting. Minnie! She was one of the inner group of these, whose not so recent release from therapy with a pass was noted. The released friends group were getting along outside. The group-friendship of the released inner group was cohesive, which is how it worked out so well. They gave passes to a group of friends so they'd stick together in success of their party. Now, Minnie, she was a person hanging around in a pavilion by a table with a coffee in her hand and some of her friends, similarly, about her. Some of those friends of hers released feelings at group therapies that offered milk therapy, those whose attributes were being human friendly, found it paid to be friendly. And all, in their way, were friendly.

"Well it is a simple attitude of being there," said Bonozy, "So friendship flourishes."

There they were! So in all of them there was an attitude, which was sure in that it was an attitude of extreme thought.

"They had said so!" said Minnie.

"So all the think tank participants are released now.!" said Mimi.

She was getting ill, deathly ill.

"In a generally overbearing assumption of security of the collective subconscious of recently released people." commented H. smartly.

"But we all are from the applicable times, which are stimulating as an unseen side." Added Bonozy.

He wore his dress smartly, uniform pants and shirt, odd shoes. And he was so humane! Athletes who offered them spare change were boons to their time.

And indeed, this took up some of their time. After heaping on them. Would helping them out with some spare change, Drony said, "This is the last of my cash pinch until next week."

Time passed and it was several seasons later. The ex stoners hung out for a short hour. A group of athletes casually strolled near the group at the park. They are from a football team practice. Some had just come from learning to play football (Varsity Football) after school and sometimes at night. They would go to practice in the evenings where the cold wind, a very strong wind, blew. Their kneecaps shook and shivered on the sidelines. They had been in many football drills on the field.

Over years, then, they had developed the physical requirements for the game. And taken to physical conditioning for the game was to be the life framework, granted with mentality and educational skills.

Boozy and Mim had gotten good at athletics before group and milk therapy, and would be most obvious in their relaxed development from it, which was still of a necessity to do something athletic.

Boozy, deathly aware, and the others were quiet for those few moments as they strolled on by tossing a ball.

"Boy! In that time to come, Boozy, I will be in front of you. You will be happy to have me as your friend, you will be relieved you know me."

"That was so far from the question of which comes first, the chicken or the egg?" said Minnie.

That's when they decided to join their friends outdoors, a part of the park they had not gone to before, an aquarium open for free sometimes and this was one of those nice days. The large swimming pools were aquariums, with a lot of types of fish.

Boozy, the possible paranoid jumped.

Seven

- Another Time Another Hail At the Aquarium

The weather was mild those intro years before 2002- from 1994.

The drawing nigh classmate of adult school, who had admired a girl and all but still gawked at her, wondered if staying pretty much a couple was best. And having the punch to survive in the long run would be good. The friend who took them home dropped them off. Boozy and the other girl and then the girlfriend last. And then they were a while after that over at the apartment in that time which were otherwise safe.

As Boozy spoke, he relaxed.

He said, "I wasn't good at it, I had tried to drive it in the same neighborhood with one way or the other, me and my close friends were for an awesome pause and admiration of the city lights and ambience, pausing at the beach in the gloom seemed a natural thing to do."

"Then, as time rolled on the released crew came up and near our homes, this tie sent most of us back to the pad, for it was time rolling on." added Buzzy.

Nonetheless, budgeting had rewarded them by a spare change mental complex where the amount multiplied.

Items score in schizoid, maniacal step, interesting, estimating, allowed thinking, way with vain aspirations, postage total, grocery items, items listed, panned out.

Boozy said, "I thought of it as if it were of a simple matrix."

Mimi commented, "Surprising, a resumption of the generalizing in processed, purchased and ongoing experience is unexpected, and slightly integral with an individual's budgeting time."

It was fruitless talking to a vacant breeze. A car pulled up. It was Dr. Portini.

Dr. Portini commented, "The hailer would be around somewhere."

"Don't be wasteful! Even insand preliminary budget writing is only slightly further away from the relationship, though it was a fantasy." said the hailer on hearing himself referred to.

Next budget, shrunken.

"The psycho therapeutic effect reduced if it down. I'll be check up on that from April-May to June." said Minnie.

The accident happened, it was good to still have the car afterwards.

Minnie long rapped, "None of me had the long time with Boozy that the others had. Neither was he into it, nor would he be by two in the afternoon. By passing to acquaintanceship with him, the psychopathic criminality of it was, as it was giving me reciprocals mentality, that he was letting it pass. This heightened my psychotic emotional add a stress, so by doing it at the time it was well, which was when others bugged us it was fault. It was for me going from one Insurance receipt to another. Soon, I'm finished paying for some of the car body repairs so the car, which I recently had got retired, got me home. It would be given to a friend."

"It was your kind of time, getting a camera and shooting." replied Bonozy. With the time getting comfortable for my total accident recall, I was all but going to be anyone anymore. Too risky. For public roads in the mountains, it was bye-bye." said Mimi.

"So I had it." replied Minnie. "And as I was going to work out in my not so straight a timeline, I said, at this time in my pursuit of happiness money and marriage to whom it would be, a person I would seek help from, I rested. The first person that was our family pastor had been a loneliest known person. I was missing from meeting him, frequently. But in my wrecked car we'll align ourselves to each other, he said. I called it on that and included my bill."

Dr. Portini declared, "A new car wrecked! And records are that finality is there such that it was something like that time when it happened before. At the time, it happened."

Leo and his brother, Logan who had not been with his brother for a while, came.

Logan said. "I'm relapsing."

Boozy, the hail bum he was, called out.

He said, "Yes, Leo. Say, Logan. How are you?"

There in the great, graduated about resume nice house of which was with it and unconditional go back status. One of as my house pasted we mostly to be super for some. And his going on I was aware of slogans in reinforce my ideas and head and by myself what I was doing there was happening like I thought about all that existed had lose weight here I might try to speed up all thought I had taken some pain at rows it'll be a long time before we are such a of the that had. It was not meant to be taken by a single person and that conversation. So it was that I was unlimited realize that wasn't right right down a real involvement with who i was everyone back home with my move in time. Bonozy came again.

Bonozy said, "I'll return to hail one on hailing day, I'll be well the above, the alcove where they park their bodies on time.

"Once I was financed to go leave all my personal property to leave." said Minnie, scared to death, in retrospect.

Previously, before it's needs a few years suppose experience told of the media you're going to the fiasco that moved away from the jail home had all from.

- The Earth Aquarium

"Tectonic plates deep under the ground, were feared to come up." Zong said.

Some ex stoners were particularly fearfully of the event, and told of rainbows that were to anyone's guess prepare one for the event. It was well onto which was going to drop into the crack from timely earth movements. The patches of grass sod, could be next.

Someone like Minnie, who was perpetually delusional actually lined up with the possibility and slept in her car in front of the party house. Minnie thought she had better stay where she was just in case it happened_____-.

Tectonic plates, further considered Buzzy delusionally, were underneath the grass sod, which were of its looseness. And he further thought, they could not be included in a downfall of the coffeehouse nor be included with the tectonic plates. His instincts were to return to the grass sod which were taken to their existence. They were before they had dropped to the level of disturbing tectonic plates. It was the fishy water view and Boozy wasn't there. He came.

And Marnie and Mae, Boozy and Bonozy sat above the glass windows of the aquarium and reminisced of the death, tectonic plates and stuff.

Banozy was scared to death that a sea creature would appear from cracks in the earth from an earthquake, and before dying bite him. Death that way was a reason to seek help. They all moved to inland villages.

Still they came and Minnie had gone and sat outside by the ocean ponding, which was like an aquarium.

In the outdoors on a cast cement bench they sat like the three classic monkeys of the familiar saying, hear no evil, speak no evil, see no evil. A breeze was blowing, but not that strongly. Boozy would have been speak no evil, Bonozy, who was new then, was like the see no evil, and Minnie hear no evil.

They had been underground visiting the aquarium world through the glass windows. Animated shows underwater portrayed a mermaid, who stayed underwater. The mermaid's prop was breathing from a tube that worked the air into bubbles so it would seem to have to surface if it were dancing with the fauna pulsating and other fishes. It was quiet! Minnie was impressed. They stayed interested as a trainer fed small fish and entertained by swimming peacefully around the mermaid.

Other aquatic creatures, all well fed, lurked in the far background of the huge fish pool that was right beside a low canyon with a creek in it.

"We had moved on and with moving were keeping up with old friends. We lived in an uncrowded neighborhood." Minnie said as she had arrived!.

After a while, they left single file, to the aquarium.

"I might have expected a porpoise to swim by." said Bonozy when they were out of there.

"Porpoises have been known to swim, occasionally close to turtles and other fish of the deep. In those clean pools, it's shallow looking but goes down to in water fountaining waters. A stingray could have been somewhere. You know, a shark is a rare creature to check out." added Bonozy.

Minnie and Mimi were soon to arrive to the benches up top in the outdoors this partly cloudy, breezy day. Mimi had sandwiches to share. Boozy arrived and set his trumpet down on the bench beside him. Shade was given by a large, well buttressed umbrella. With both of them talking, Boozy and Boozy were watching them. They were like panelists, yet they were friends.

Minnie commented, "Time is moving on." She had, in that, at least been concerned about their next meals.

Mimi retorted, "It was so far from . . . exist. I had . . . almost all the money I needed to exist on for a while. And it helped Monnie. If I would be given some more, Mimi? I could call you on my phone if I would be so okay."

Tomorrow would come. Mimi helped Minnie out before she could help herself.

Mimi said, "Her friend is out again."

Their time next to the aquarium went next to inside--underneath.

The cafeteria room faced one of the solid glass sides of the aquarium. A slow, big fish watched through the glass as they had eaten, other fishes, some as big, some bigger ambling about were nearby.

The next thing, someone has a car. The car.

"I had a job. . ." He said.

"Tomorrow would come, I would be okay." said Minnie.

"I had been informed of a new car for sale, and getting this one would make it less need to hitchhike. It needed a good paint job and I had a job so could by scrimping, get the new paint job."

The car, which had an inclination to veer rightward because the rubber on its tires were worn to a side, had a steering linkage looseness from overly long bolts being used to hold it together, by the previous owner, who repaired cars. The natural play in the steering made it suitable for excitement driving, impulse steering and road rage, though it was the car's fate to have a flat tire.

Boozy continued, "I was getting good at tuning up my car.

Buzzy replied, "But I could never tune my truck."

There was a pause and Minnie looked hard trying to make sense of it.

Buzzy paused, then continued, "My job was once at a used car lot. And this used car, which kept my skill at tuning in an it's getting better mode, was for sale. So I bought it.

Later, by many years, the car was owned by a relative through a friend of the previous owner. I went from safety check to safety check. Okay! I had a meeting with them; and I was processing the registration form correctly!"

There was a pause and he continued, almost ruminating.

He said, "According to you, this was just in time for me to take my friend with me to a major rock concert."

"Bonozy, you're okay." answered Mimi.

She was as good a friend in friendship one might have. Bonozy continued his rhetorical rambling to joy of them all. It was certainly an interesting conversation.,

Mimi talked up, "Back with their playing records on their record player, all in friendship, I had no idea then that the music was country. We were into anti-war songs and powerful lead guitar riffs."

"You ruminating?" asked Boozy fruitlessly.

"No idea?" asked Miimi.

"It was in my being a senior worker there for a year, and that was like a scene. I'd get there after working."

"As what?" asked Mimi in a joyous way.

Boozy and his older brother, who was dimwitted and went away to a school, were special for those kind of kids. They enjoyed being there and this went beyond with Leo and his brother who had studied hard, going away from the dimwit school to be nonetheless, at once, employable.

In the front of their seating at this studio, a time talking to another guy who had dropped by, he knew Leo and Logan and said so.

He said, "For real? Are you guys really going to push the back of my chair?"

Bonozy said, "I think not. And don't go so loud. I don't want anybody more to hear us."

It would be a long rolling year before going home. He went to many concerts and just up and yelled like he was sure that he was in a concert himself.

Boozy commented, "It was crazy."

It was drizzly and cold with endless wind storms and so the all encompassing march of rain squalls, which were part of the storms, blew through the open window of the outer porch.

The small accident happened after the car had been paid for.

Doug, an old friend of Leo's, who had come to a party and decided not to go oin, was there.

He said, "I was apparently accident prone and being in an accident, a victim of several times up to that point, where I would again come to great proportions of shock and pain. Yet, as I was unaffected by it as far as I was concerned, and it wasn't too long a look after graduating up to a truck from a car, which was higher off the ground in a school of expertise, having reduced the car to rubble in an accident, which I had been prone to avoid, I know how it is."

"It was but my basic knowledge of the matter." added Minnie. "Besides word of mouth there and then, there was a loud oral report of someone, who gave up in relating a class of accident events, some were about television reporting and some were radio programs reporting on it. the accident was still somebody's thing."

"In a yard where they were renting, it served for a campsite for some of us," said Doug, "more local times passed as I was gravitating to the more home type and family."

"It came as the lifestyle was not occurring to me and was something to do as getting by on the meager income, perhaps went to serious business." said Bonozy.

Then there was that friendship stress emotion delusion.

6 The Doctors, and

- They were wrapping up year end when new year coming prep.

"Especially good to be here." cried Mimi.

Anyone else from then on thought the special mental telepathy message was as a rehab invitation.

"People from the aquarium and tectonic plate virtual reality have significance; yet this was one it about having from that see" said Minnie.

She was still scared to death that they'd find out she was okay with some of the things going on. Psychotic guest she was, arriving with the stuff to have a good time was it.

Minnie commented, "And I never told anyone before going to the airport wondering if it had given some bad advice."

"Who were you to be dropped to a concert?" Mimi asked.

It was soon another mental telepathic event without mental telepathy.

April was a strange time, in retrospect time. It was it, was on a promise that of which I remember so little of that my rock star companion to me from the psychotic of mental telepathy.

The party going to be it will be - the other companion she was supposedly arriving than arriving sometime and definite she will be coming and I guessed arriving to I thought it was definite and I never told anyone before going.

"Park my car," said Dr. Portini. "A convertible."

He would stop and go.

It will still to be a few more weeks before they would leave to meter in time.

Would it be to mountains? Or/and it was. And then probably was a normal down time. Boozy was there and driving a car.

"I want to try divining." said Boozy.

"I dove into some of my more familiar subjects and more, but that which had been given to me by a boss acronym with code my high-school teacher had been then I was sensitive to fumes." replied Minnie, scared to death that her boyfriend would find out she had been somewhere unusual.

"I will from the book I carried in my coat pocket. and here I was,"

Boozy continued walking, reading and thinking. An old attachment served him in the idea this has to come as a pillow to stress. And he had his other friends, some of whom were dear.

Boozy and Minnie to cushion his shouldering a lot of endeavors. As he went a round into the tie of friendship, they were restful.

"To try to not do materializing is to get up." said Doug.

"I was admitted to a town get together, where a close relationship ensued." commented Bonozy.

"Being in a union and thinking there is a mental ward union, a friend had reported a similar psychotic town time experience, was fortunate." Doug interjected.

Eight

"It was late November 2008.

Minnie commented, "And I was going to go through the terminal lobby at the town owned airport."

"Sure." said Mimi.

She went on to this group therapy counselor in private.

Mimi said, "I listen to Zong, she got an album out and I took it to a room in a house where I was living. I was a working student, psyched up to stay at a junior college but hesitant to be glad that the album happened. That much is a lot of words. It was a collection of some sing along songs and the music had all so much to it."

Dr. Portini replied, "Are you comfortable that happened?"

"And Buzz was trying to sleep in the living room." she responded. "He really needed his sleep."

Also, Boozy was typing some of his school papers, so much for having no work and over limit of credit hours.

"Life with good roommates had one of many good points. We talk for a little while and do our thing. Word was, one of the roommates latest music efforts included Minnie's music."

This was after a year or two of the supportive efforts. So one semester life t manifested missed as my taking off a few more credits he retrieved them."

"This was alright living to me." said Bonozy.

It seemed at times I wasn't really very well acquainted with. But until my final exit, they of the house are, uh, fine!"

And customer friendly fellow, who had seen much along the line, may have once."

One must always try and be with tricks of the trade's and had the psychotic work.

"Of psychotically working, I have been thinking friend the helped I was to be surprised when he turned out to be a friend who could maybe have a doctor helping him have a fiasco in psychosis bliss.

"Had he completely been as last he had been and ended up with an, it wasn't nice with a nice and very there this was highlighted, I have been lightly fidgeting."

"I had a little or something I was into a school and had I and a friend had done a little psychotic experimenting with film. Psychotic movies and psychotic ideals at school psyched, and there and I was still telling it into my home school activities painting had been and had over one hundred. I have quite a painting on the association floor. It was psychosis plus subconscious so 'still home' where I was thinking of time off. Which was it, thinking psychotically, or 'I have preposterous psychotic thoughts of what the real psychopathic story behind the landlord's family has been'."

"We were lucky we talked psychology as much as we did." added Boozy. "Some time or another, we tried for and got it when had we may have done what you could hear. Psychosis accelerating by the shape at the back end of the valley from an old lady we associated around with."

Minnie rattled on, "We add to another on time at a rogue alley house. Our state of being is, we know. And then we played some music. We are psychotic. And everything that we left at the rogue house was for them, it was there, and it's psychosis." commented Buzz with stand up exertion to expound.

And yet it seemed that he was becoming more and more together in my psychotic mind and to be for them. So with that and friends being liked, before it was like it had been a long time ago when I seem to feel a little wasted a lot of them I'm at a road, halfway to my place and gone for a while."

"I had but was it ended shortly after I got robbed my psychotic experience was psychotic job just like that and it seemed good always. but then I would be leaving tomorrow night so it seemed suddenly it works in the little to put up with probably been apart of it I seem to get a lot of it."

One couldn't tell nor did I know but end of the successes of psychosis seems to be.

This was a lot of concern.

Boozy started again, "Then, perhaps I do some art. certainly it worked psychotic to my investments of time would pay off and in the little success was psychosis gratification- and you should be a success enough to does a large amount of work. I had yet to do that to achieve success. It was something else. Relationship wasn't necessary. but then my would be coming along with me probably for their success.

"Uh huh!" said Minnie.

Boozy went on, "If it was up to me, and perhaps that would make me or him want to wake up, me, I go up to see the hailer. And you go later. It was right and knew it.

"I knew I would be working again but there was no job there, even though it seemed to come up to an, if a psychosis mad someone denied family and psyched out they would be sick.:

"I would have to agree with you. If I had really been stuck with that, and if there was a coincidence.

"I know you have said I had just read about one's man's attempt to relationship union. in a book I was reading over and over perhaps a connection with psychotic paint abuse. had and psychopathic violence were connected. I looked at the had recently. All supposed to have rules for school back up and my relationship couldn't put a bond.

So, so, so very psychotic and so shiny and psych it to the circulator rotating board over cylinder. we're still working from my it so fifteen yards or.

"So I will sitting days one day when the doctor's assistant walked in and said something psychotic., and we panicked. then had I hope there's no had last cell once used sold apartment of line.

Identification of gender mindset as well as personality is for those who want identification of gender orientation.

"Image design and perhaps psychotic identification crises psychoses, which have led me to dictate eradicate rules, rules my usual life." said Minnie seriously.

Boozy looked at her and thought of all the places he'd been where if she had gone with him, it would have been unusual to hail someone.

Boozy hailed the nearest party goer.

"Hey." he said loudly.

"At the time of your psychosis and infatuation for title of psychoses queen, you get half psycho and suggest there's a scene where you can go to a far away land. It seems ro be a lineup, then you seem too prepped up to cross the barrier into reality." replied Minnie.

"This may be true." he replied, then connecting to his gut pit core vital energy center, not too loudly he continued his hailing, "Hey." There was silence for a moment and he hailed again, "You."

She was the only one around that she could see. But there was someone in the shadows of night light tree blocks nearby.

Someone in the background of the party said, "So you go psyched up; and that has grabbed me as tattle telling thing/"

A group therapy later and Boozy was better. Lately, a mind kit gender identity positions one to maybe not be the kind of thing to tell uninformed people. If the end of rock and roll song came and had died out, its gender identification could have done away with the death impacts from intoxication, that taking on new meaning and going away from the identification of gender.

Zong, who appeared after a long absence, came up to dealing with the post stoner episode and repentance. She says that death just doesn't have anything to do with it, even when she was talking about her friend Minnie to Bonozy.

She said, "Why couldn't you be good?" Mimi asked.

"Always so into being into that antipsychotic psychotherapy." Borony replied.

Zong was there and robotically replied, "But I have not entered the wildest dream psychoanalysis. In psychosis, whether it's true or not, intoxication makes a difference to most everyone except you. You have to be in the area of mental health or should be. So much for a draft of hard liquor."

A lot of time passed when they stood there with their jaws dropped, looking like they'd gone into a suspended.

Minnie commented, "If you're gone past when I was to measure my regular girlfriend. If she hadn't had cosmetic surgery along the line of cover-up and that was before I had never heard before my life over the years have been. Friday flighty but not only I did find it difficult to maintain a job psych but every thought I had was cut short while after the link street according to my source of for-show. Me, I go to my other psychotic historical figures. I would never mess with a plaid for love. and I found up psychotic-drunk on the floor but I've never known a woman who could take me to when I was ok."

And at the same time they feel like you know how much to leeway with a drunkard hailer.

The card then come put up with me and that's how I had been starting out but don't have a way of reappearing.

"How are you?" asked the doctor.

She answered, "Psychosis? You tell me."

"Okay, I'll tell you. You're overly nervous."

"For me it seemed better to add less to the conversation. But when he asked me if it was okay to ask me something I considered what I was thinking."

"That could do it to you.: the doctor replied.

She went on, "So it could happen soon, I'll be hailed soon as the chance comes."

The doctor said, "Then, we will all be well."

The receptionist commented, "I'm writing a personal letter. From me to you, I'm writing to a love, it's with an I will think about a continued hail of a love, a love of a psyched talent."

They didn't pay any attention to the receptionist. In fact, the doctor swung the open door closed and sneered at the receptionist he was paying to keep outsiders out. It was empty in the waiting room and the receptionist looked glum.

Mimi gave one of her long statements, "Some of those types of things, which you never share are a psychotic word. Neither hailer, nor one to be there would be here, nor would an always possessed.

"We were never possessed by the participants." said Doctor Portini.

And no one came into the empty waiting room.

The receptionist was there.

She went on, "Other things would undoubtedly be left to anyone's guess but some things that were here were good. They were possessions. And, you know all were all but cool with psychotic information. Neither was psychic information good.

"The exclamations of a hailing someone change.

The hailer entered and sat down got comfort

He said, "I am one who could deserve more of a nice time than I'm getting."

"Sure." said the receptionist.

Nobody else was around.

Hailer Bum went on, "I'd like time off from a psychotic examination with this explanation, that's all I ever get, examination with an explanation. The doctor looked stark and at me and he tells me what psychotic things his clients say. The clients are worse than me, he says. To me, it's all but a day of work an honest dollar, all of course of out of and into psychoanalysis therapy. I knew some psychoanalysis could help. Then it was okay. And if it could help, but I'm just a client, I'd rather be a receptionist."

The receptionist looked at her with thoughtful eyes. There were a few minutes of quiet there besides the air conditioning.

But what is the probability that one of those clients would wish the receptionist was closer to them. The client Hail Bum was all but into a bummer.

Hail Bum said, "It is up me to come into love psychosis with the main receptionist?"

"I'm no sex therapist." she answered. "If you want, I'll tell you how to relax."

Hail Bum answered quickly, "Lie down." He was sarcastic. Some psychotic once said to me, lie down once. Now, I'm someone else who perhaps is coming to see a doctor to get therapy. Some client says to me, I like you. Now I'm into a therapy? Who wants a name change the client asked me? Have we worked out with others? Fortunately, no. But knowing my probabilities well enough it doesn't matter. She probably likes me so much it's to hard to be truthful and admit they're half dumb, too crazy to be much at math. Not so much of an okay person with me. Best to avoid that line of thought, I nod. I say, hey. I'm not hailing you like a street barker in front of a night club. As it might come up. I find out this one is has a twisted male-female gender psychosis, gender partnershipping psych is a sort of way out for one of them. They're that way. That's why they come to see the doctor.

"So what have you been happening to move on to? Life a little delicious? Like I have one person more into my time other than more than one, I think it's an open door with a way there. That's really started me getting by with the psychosis going by. Believe that's only in my favor."

Mimi slipped into the waiting room and heard some of the nice receptionist's ruminating and talking to herself. Mimi wondered if the receptionist, Joann had been on something herself.

Mimi sat, waited and added, "I have moved from one room to another. And it's a not a change of psychosis. It's a change for me. I have everything I needed and a good song.

It was like putting butter on your bread, handling psychosis. Everybody's got it. It gets you so if you cracks a question behind the dish that's being served to you in a restaurant, it's changing behind your mind, which needs dusting, and comes out a statement on something the person they were talking to could use."

Doctor came in the room.

"Your head kept pushing me as a professional student." he said to "I was psyched, working so I could plan on that I will graduate with a degree in psychopathic psychosis having move to a larger room my new room headspace there's going final not too long before I moved and in their own that regenerate to psychosis and be just laugh it off talk to myself and said if I use your written notes for hours.

"Do you have to scream?" asked Marnie.

"You were screaming unspeakable idiocies, Bonozy." reported Seth.

The friendly Dr. and Mimi screamed in glee and alternating unison expectation, in after which the scream died down.

Boozy replied, "I wonder if you would wonder what I was talking about? If I were you, I'd be polite."

And that really set Mimi and the doctor back a bit, back to a group therapy consciousness. The doctor. was suddenly especially cautionary.

"I would really like to know what that was all about?" Doctor Rodgers asked. "It's being a top occurrence should be helpful? Do we usually scream in glee? No, Bonozy. But we were just discussing your trumpet playing and it was that good."

Mae added, "A good thing is for you to do, Tony, is to stop and ask us if we really need to scream like that."

"And j was asking myself, why are psychoses like that happening? Is it like negative schizophrenia.?" Dr. Portini added.

Boozy made a point, "It was good, I told you. It was so loud! When I was listening to music, perhaps I was upset with the world in which I live, and I was letting it go, I kept it quiet. Now you keep screaming. But if it was up to me, I'd prefer it a little less loud. It has to become accustomed to a thing."

Zong, who was sitting a bit to the side was very psyched up by the screaming to make some more money as is his case. He is the esteemed Zong., who can come up with schemes and make the money. He's from the far country, experienced at mountaineering, keen of jungle hiking, and had enjoying the nature of our world. As it was, he was saying things.

He said, "It's that good to be in the place where I live."

He stood up.

"Sit down, Mr. Zong." replied the doctor adamantly. "Living is the force of natural psychosis, which is okay in if it doesn't go too far."

Mae added, "No, he didn't care if you're dr. or you called him a psychotic. We're about to scream because we like the weather. Therefore, I know if I would scream it or not. Wouldn't a good scream keep me working on my own psychoses calming?"

Doctor Portini commented, "As much as I am a part of that, I will try and forget it."

"It has to be edited from the right side of my brain." replied Borony.

"This memory? Has it been me and you in a dream?"

He shakes his head okay.

"And it was just what I was saying," went on Dr. Portini "If we're even just willing to do the right thing it's going to be okay."

Sarcastically, Boozy answered. "So do a stylistic antipsychotic thing like scream? I laugh. Dr., Portini, are you okay?"

"I see. Then there will be a next time, a good time."

"Am I right? I thought so. You stay okay."

"I suppose it would all be about the same difference in a house?"

"Yes it would. And to some extent it would be better than the same. So let that may be a lesson."

"Let's go ask the clock doctor, Doctor?"

Dr. Portini's doctor entered and said, "In that, I am your dr., you had me introduced to an interesting yoga mindset discipline. Laugh."

"Then we have ten minutes." commented Dr.

"Time in which we stand like an island in the sea, laughing our fool heads off at the abundance, I am of the majority."

"You psychotic non laugher. Laugh. It's good for you."

"Ha, ha. There, Doctor"

"They have got it." said Dr. Then they all laughed.

"All of the collective subconscious groups have psychoses." Boozy said. "So with another collective subconscious, laugh consciousness, it's for a highly beneficial moral majority collective subconscious."

We are in a majority, Boozy." said Doctor Portini. He laughed. His laughing went on for ten minutes.

"On cue of laughter, Bonozy, if you went into a psychotic mindstate the doctors would relax at it's occurring and have his fading laughter."

They sat, with expressions of familiarity to their mind as Bonozy, in a place of regular happiness.

He said, "Wasn't bad in the good old days, which everyone even the longtime friend Buzzy, who manages to pop up and deliver on his promises, been a bother. He has more psychoses than me."

Dr. Portini asked, "So he has an expanse of time that is moot? Did you like the earthquake?"

Dr. Rodgers finally chirped in, "We are laughing and screaming so as to be mentally healthy."

He laughed. It seemed a while the doctors was going on and laughing, Tony giving everyone directions on why to laugh was stretching it, but before they knew it this one weekend, the doctor left. He and Doctor Rodgers had jumped in this red sports car and with a waggy hi-ho, off we go, went with arm motions like someone clearing the air. They drove off. Presumably back to a rehab gab to laugh it off.

One or the other of those who hailed Bonozy requested to be identified.

I need her for personal attention a birthday party and hadn't been quite the same so I remembered having gotten psyched working come to. I guess yoga with cultural hand had been offering but this had been much of the continuum.

"I was getting some place real. when I went to her birthday party they had a television message from person and psychotic country where he was feeling an elephant sized psychosis with chocolate. So I would be amazing.

"I had enjoyed being in a room I'm go there and ready for this coming to take my hand regularly undo it was unfortunate that it was that was finally getting the bus with me as I have benefited if I hadn't changed room."

Saying things might have been different in the end, but it didn't matter.

"So it wouldn't matter to me if I was mostly interested in working at something."

Yet they psyched up to hear all that some good was going on.

"To us, saying she ratted and all was illusive. And that had almost got me wondering, if it wasn't some sort of psychotic psychic, uh, setup, which it was.

"But any cool we had that was so bad to the outcome was another thing. In thinking, which satisfied its end results. There were, overridden by the fact that I had just answered an ad for it in the first place, great promises.

"For something and much more unexpected would likely happen. Whatever! I might have done was part of the package, it was good as done, and so many other job orientations.

"Whatever ones that I had lunch with that were well off made me say, then I'm sorry. I've been up since early and it leaves me there with those early risers, who go so energetically all day."

Thrifty as that was, one could and did speed out getting dressed. When one inserted themselves in their clothing to enjoy, they relaxed.

"It, then, as it seems my neighbors from will show that he was leaving I didn't mind that much it seemed that be able to perhaps I suppose my personality had a lot to be considered aggressive and a passive sort of way I had once in awhile when but did have a

"I could not say positively what he had said or meant he was like so many psychotic drunks are and it's just been playing some sort of line game it seemed rich when I asked him what he did I think it one time someone it should have been on a bummer, though.

Death wonders if, when there isn't some mental telepathy going on with the hailers, if thought is there. He thought, I can use extrasensory perception too.

Death was an expounded on experience.

Boozy said, "I wondered if it was possible that there was some sort of psychotic ESP psych happening? Then! Did I? Could it be factual my being there and with my thinking psychosis as mental telepathy was something? I looked for what should be traveling on there, not to what it was, but if there, to a lot of friendship. Once, out of my stay at a new place, it was a quasi intellectual."

Eventually, I have which is so unfortunately I might make an exception and have the general peanut butter on the side. It is an exception I don't know what to do with it. I finally was told, will it end up I'm psyched up and working for the, ever in a treasured friendship, man?

"They are all is it might be there is no good my tools over right around about my eyes are tired change the light sleep maybe an escape psychotic suggestions and then none to sound is there"

"Assess it at the park voice with a friend but I heading out of the office was song. I prayed we have come to love.

Bonozy said, "So I didn't call the carpool today!" When he get there so the two sports what happened in traffic, I had played a good tire in a similar situation when it was funny. has been there too long then there it is all over either way both times make and dang the merchandise not still with her business involvement. And then we were there in paradise. There, there was nothing to there. Then, of course, there's there was nothing to say. She moved out right. Didn't go right. And I forgot my friends-with-friends care after a time or so, So I'm around the house."

"Really nice to room in the place. Yet if I think right from the start, I think, mind state."

"I'm back to words of authority boiling me. They're to see if I'm onto the similarities and differences that exist. But to no end. And eventually I have to face up to that, which is served in conversation. And fortunately they make an exception."

You dictating or something?" asked Mimi. Boozy was.

Boozy dictating was his off the wall ruminating like rap, "The little woman in living room or kitchen! It sounds so relaxing. if they are in an entirely different direction I know trucks don't have eyes. when are Rows 2? we set to go I had thought I had a few more days go by but I meant to set the alarm I meant to pull the button and then after lunch before I made a very important discovery which was working add nothing to do and I'm take care of everything I'm doing from medicines to all sorts of Health on also the things wrong with me I'm working if that's not enough I'm feeling worse so to say the least it means more medicine go and not to mention but your eyes were above except for its better than I think later I have some I'm not doing too well so end or always well then, I think I am; I believe I can return to the radio with the news and all of that." He is saying, on it.

"You can say that." said Mimi quickly, then, to let him know she was there.

Bozony went on, "It has a few things for me I'm back to relaxing until I feel drowsy so I check the telephone to see if it's okay there is no name check and which is time we some at early afternoon my moral is don't count your chickens until they hatch the weather comes in on the radio and I go into automatic relaxation with board it's all relative."

Time caught up with them and they had to ask for spare change.

Death was comfortable with that.

Mimi, feeling comfortable with his friends, Tooty and Mini entered the cabin door to its living room and started a discourse again. It was good for which he was famous for,

Mimi said, "Personally!"

There was a long pause.

The ring of schizophrenics was a small one. Minnie, who had just survived a bout with his shadow, sat next to Tony, recovering from having fallen on a steps, slipping on an old stained spot wet from rain. Seth was welcomed.

He limped, recovered some from a turn of the ankle, to one of two empty slightly cushioned chairs. The ring grew by one.

Bonozy, recovering from his personally statement, which had left them listening, said, "The psychosis of schizophrenia is schizoid ego, an effect too delusional. So mere thinking, we're thinking!

Spare change could seem like group therapy.

In economics people and people are growing group therapy theory.

"May I say." commented BUzz, interested in having his spare change loaned out and returned, "You are riding on the debt." Time is your time off, no interest, while riding on the debt.

"This is one dimensional," he continued.

"Friends, this is your demand that creates demand."

"Okay." replied the man, a little demandingly, "So if my cost is four dollars and something cents, my spare change I gave, and I've got five dollars to eat out, my pocket money is no more than ten dollars. That I've got to spend."

He thinks he's compelled by delusion and almost motivation to spend. To spend what he's got, so to have enough money, he goes to his bank and withdraws two times what he has got to spend to have enough. In pocket money.

It's the third day after he withdrew his money and he's having a zippy breakfast. This was schizophrenia pretty much beyond the one dimension debt riding time. He's thinking he should go vertical in time to start a time of an observation; so some of that wayout euphoria mnemonic doctor makes sense ensues. And helps avoid the pressure of realities.

So, he gulped down his milk tea latte, paying out two and a half dollars and spare cents.

Boozy tells him, "Deposit time, big spender."

There's a few moments when nobody knows what to do because they've never heard of this before. Boozy looked around before sitting down.

They sit-in in a way, a bit of the way toward a round at a round table. They sit there and have their zippy breakfasts.

Minnie knew a lot about the host there and commented.

Minnie said, "Let's have another round."

The round table was empty. Nobody seemed to know how it got there. It was bigger than a bread basket and couldn't have fit through the door. It was perfectly found and allowed parties to exist on opposite sides.

Bonozy says, "Let them milk you. Leave a tip."

He lays eighty-five cents next to his plate like he's trying to hide something. Boozy slaps a dollar down next to his empty cup and Dobby and Hugo both leave two dollars each.

Not every one of the gang, the gang that went out to score a tablet, would go to Milk therapy. The ones that did liked it. The others went their way.

Boozy walked into Dr. Porini's office, even the receptionist was not present, and sat down. He was thinking, I'll do this before I get into that hypno-milk therapy. I'll do a thing by asking when they come in, or come back.

They would come back!

Dr. Portini was first in from having a coffee break with his receptionist, Miss Alri. They were fresh.

Dr. Portini asked, "How did you get in."

Boozy replied, "The door was unlocked so I came right on in."

Miss Airi added, "I must have left the latch off. Glad you've got your office double locked."

"Ya, me too."

"Nothing out here but some comfy seats and a counter with a telephone and buzzer for your office."

"It could be alright. Tell my client to come in, milk therapy starts in five minutes."

Mini said, "Alright."

"You Boozy. Wait a few minutes. Sorry no one was here when you came in. Thank you for waiting. The doctor will be right with me."

Boozy was a strange cat. She liked to dress male, but she adhered to the strictures that say, the best females are the ones that dress male. Her mates all agreed.

Now, that some time had passed, it was the year 2004 and she was recommending Dr. Portini and his Center for Milk Therapy to her friends. She had seen Dr. Portini a few times.

Milk therapy was a long ways off for Mimi and her friend.

She would come to enjoy milk therapy. It would help. It could help. She could find her way in life to milk therapy sessions with a special, good doctor.

Milk therapy would be in the picture for Mimi and others of her very small gang.

Nine

She'd had tried psychedelics, and went the exhaustive route and wound up wondering if she should go rehabbing. Mimi liked many rehab offers and knew she'd eventually pick up on one. She went and returned and tried another rehab.

She, like so many others, wondered if she were going into phase two psychedelic use. Some of her friends were definitely into phase two psychedelic use. Some of Mimi's friends surpassed the some of her friends who were into psychedelic phase two use and who got into phase three psychedelic use.

She was smart and witty. The oldest quote she knew was from a book about someone careful about their intake, someone who was getting away from it all. She was up there on her info, gung ho to prove that it was good to be careful with life surviving skills. Smart as to what she used and its sources was Mimi.

The next year when group therapy came up for her, she had been enjoying some hot disco. The party ended with a blind date where she backed out at the last moment after dinner.

She, like most of her friends were getting by okay. Some of her acquaintances and the passers-by who wanted an occasional hand out could get the recommendation to see the doctor.

Mimi said, "Go see Dr. Portini. I've seen him for years. You'll not be sorry or worse off if you see Dr. Portini."

Boozy, one of her newer acquaintances, who had some experience was a stoner, was sceptical.

Boozy said, "I drank. I drink. Ya, I use safe drugs sometimes. Substance use for me is very light, sporadic, and safe. I used more than once medicinally inclined recreational drugs, for my good mental health and for the most part in which guilt was abuse, it was out of the picture. Use took me to years of undoing the life I was into. It took years of working on myself to get my life normal."

Mimi queried, "Smoking was a thing?"

"Yes. And I wound up with a denial complex."

Mimi quickly said, "I know this Dr. Portini."

Mimi tried to keep her friend Minnie together. She kept him on the subject of dreaming by talking about her own dreams. And Minnie admitted to using drugs to help him dream.

She was now seeing Dr. Ludd. And Minnie was in the conversation. He had considered seeing the doctor too.

She was in Dr. Ludd's consultation office and in the middle of a discussion on dream occurrence and drug use.

They would all eventually get to their therapy.

The therapist let them in and it went down like clockwork orange.

"Let me get this straight." said the doctor. "You were at a party last night and it reminded you of a party you went to two years ago and you're afraid you're going to relapse into the psychosis you had from going to that party you went to two years ago. So you came to see me."

Boozy said, "Yes."

"And you think there was maybe someone following you?"

"I found it hard to believe too."

"You know if you think someone is following you it's your insanity. I mean, you'll be the one with schizophrenia. Paranoia. Idiocy."

"I wouldn't let it get that far, doc. But it wasn't just one or two people, there was a like a funeral procession following me."

"You think if you've got paranoia you'll be better off."

"No, I wouldn't think so."

"You have got to be helped, my friend. You shouldn't see me for milk therapy, sex therapy is what you want. And if you are smart you'll get education therapy. While I'm at it, I am recommending you to group therapy. Reality therapy may help you. Also!"

"Ok."

"There, you'll meet more of your kind. There was a young lady in last week who had a similar problem.

"Scared to death of her shadow. She had done a little shadow boxing but gave up. She started coming to my group therapy. We sat around and watched a kaleidoscope on a four foot by four foot screen. It was a computerized presentation by a gifted designer, and we decide on if the kaleidoscope is designed to be an atom or a molecule. Or what kind of atom is it or what kind of molecule it is, or where the molecule is in substance. Then, what's happening in the supposed atom."

"This kaleidoscope, it is correcting my friend's Alzheimer's?"

"Said to help."

Mimi asied, "This kaleidoscope, is it correcting my paranoia?"

Doctor Portini paused before speaking, "I see it is as an imagined molecule. By going through cycles, the kaleidoscopic repeats, they go from an imagined start point, to recognized places in the kaleidoscopic vision where next to nothing is happening. Supposed molecularizations occur. If taken to so many times, the molecule is reached. The many radicals of the LSD molecule, for example, can be seen as somewhat exhaust like because of the many radicals, it can be assumed to coexist in an around view that is kaleidoscopic. They are in design but are then perfect. Count to so many changes, so many to make that molecule."

"I'd like help, doctor. But I don't want to go to outer space."

The quick doctor answered, "Hail the rocket nerd. He was the one who knew what it felt like to be himself, which was when it was like it was when it was better to be pseudonymous."

There was a general pause and he went on.

"I know. I told you to call me."

Zong said, "Hail doctor."

The doctor commented, "I was here to see about three possibilities of helping three cases. I came up with that so this was the case. Go on Mimi."

Mimi said, "Once I was born without a prostate sex gland, twice I had dreamed it out, urinated bloody discharges amid the urinary infection and three, being further operated on without my knowledge or consent in that area, was daunting my thinking. And that it was taken from me was secondary."

The next person said, "I came up with a fairly drawn out explanation for myself as being an agent in secret training, which was secret to the third agent, whose third explanation drifted into a reality for all scenario."

Mimi and Minnie were about to the park site.

Minnie said, "I had been taken at that very early age of one year old and given through micro surgery by some unauthoritative, renegade, skilled, doctor, whose group professed this was for the good of all, to be this way."

Mimi was calm and listened till she was through. Mimi thought, 'And so my prostate removed at this young ate, I was supposed to go into an imbalance of my glandular system, which made me unsuitable for further development as a secretive type gone fem secret agent'. She was with Minnie, who was especially considerate and understanding. They found their way to the doctor's gathering. The doctor had a few of his favorite clients together at an outdoor picnic area for a session. He said, "Another possibility in your mind, I suppose would be life was additional?"

Zoong said, "I had become a participant in the international exchange, which was apparently beyond my experimental suggestion, when the idea was, the third world was a family, was in danger and was in this glandular share and exchange. It was with us as a way to take us into something else."

Boozy was questioning "Another event in one's childhood is supposed, this is to have happened to take the training for the secret secret agent into supposed slightly higher degrees?"

Zong replied, "In the childhood event, which had been one to a position of above anyone entering the group someone, anyone who was entering was in a make ready mind area."

Dr. Portini priyed, "The pounce move was ingrained?"

The sleeper in the hold was a person who entered the person down on the ground, and they who had died had to be taken off to a public kitchen to work it out. The person who was in their own house, had a similar leg hold, but was replaced in process by the future looking person, who had snappy attack ingrained in them. They might possibly be directed by certain events or stimuli to be more aware of the possible vagueness of this, which was a later event that had happened to come to a more allowed blackout, the professor of this resulted in succeeding to come out of it and retaliate to turn their lights off. So an accident was supposed an accident that happened facilitated by drinking and drug use, in the drink was not accountable to them.

Supposedly this was to further facilitate the agent to have the snap attack in such situations.

Supposedly a dummy, no life person, as a condemned prisoner had been found and was being participated on to some degree by the blackout person, who was overly supposed willing to to do it. Perhaps in another case, another time, a real person being targeted.

And since they had been somewhat attacked, nonetheless a event there seemed to be the possibility that the manikin of some description was mistaken by the participant retaliation to have been used as the victim. Since there was another possibility, it was that there was a mistake in the process and someone was actually receiving the end result of the snap attack agent, which may have then supposedly occurred as a party required cover up by the resulting responsible authorities, and some had come to anti schizoid acts of blackout violence.

This wasn't alright since they may have been taking hallucinating medicines so they waited at a bus stop near where this was taking place.

One was having an imagined time and were becoming quite paranoid to some such extent, particularly of quite sharp objects appearing where cigar butts once had been, where cigar butts should have been. This was in places where they may have been likely to come up with an accidental scratch in which they themselves would become, through the course of normal physical movements, affected. These sharp objects were supposedly of auto accidents, which to say the least and according to the thoughts in those months, were of the forces there, which were supposedly from preparations that were invisible. How could invisible, harmless radar waves have an affect. And unseen. From places where that had been something suspicious, so they were wary and cautious supposing that that was the show, traffic put the objects about.

Sharp agents were planting others like themselves and planted others were from the same area.

CPSIA information can be obtained
at www.ICGtesting.com
Printed in the USA
BVHW071252010519
547057BV00005B/476/P

9 781796 028515